THE GOLDEN MÉTIS

FLYNN J. ELL

PEMMICAN PUBLICATIONS INC.

THE GOLDEN MÉTIS

Flynn Ell

Pemmican Publications Inc. gratefully acknowledges the assistance accorded to its publishing program by the Manitoba Arts Council, Canada Arts Council and the Book Publishing Industry Development Program.

Library and Archives Canada Cataloguing in Publication

Ell, Flynn J.
The golden Métis / Flynn J. Ell

ISBN 1-894717-20-1

I. Title.

PS3555.L48G64 2004 813'.54 C2004-904475-3

Cover and Book design: Sherry M. McPherson
Cover Artwork: Deanna L. Lalonde

The word Wakankanka is a contraction of Wakanyanka, one–who–sits–above–all, wife.

For my wife, Karin,
the Wakanka Woman

contents

Chapter 1	Page 1
Chapter 2	Page 15
Chapter 3	Page 27
Chapter 4	Page 45
Chapter 5	Page 59
Chapter 6	Page 71
Chapter 7	Page 85
Chapter 8	Page 103
Chapter 9	Page 119
Chapter 10	Page 135
Chapter 11	Page 151
Chapter 12	Page 165
Chapter 13	Page 181
Chapter 14	Page 197
Chapter 15	Page 213

The Golden Métis
Flynn J. Ell

Chapter 1

He was a dark, bobbing speck that broke the monotonous grey line of the horizon one moment. Then, his shape turned into a man on a cantering horse before they dropped to the dry, valley floor and dust churned behind the horse's gallop.

His long, sandy hair was knotted at the back of his head beneath a flat leather sombrero from which a single eagle feather danced in the air currents. His hair streamed from his shoulders like a silken handkerchief whenever the black piebald broke into a gallop. The man's eyes were hazel, set in a brown field of leathery skin pinched into wrinkles above his high cheekbones from squinting.

He knew he was handsome because women in the taverns he frequented sought a place by him at the bar, and he could have his way with them.

An ebony-handled, fourty-four Navy Colt bounced at his hip to the rhythm of the horse's gait. The gun was tied to his right thigh by a rawhide thong, as were his weathered buckskin jacket and bedroll tied behind the cantle where Buster bobbed. The raccoon's bandit face peered around the man's hip and over the handgun. A fringed, leather flap sealed a fourty-four Henry in its saddle scabbard, the gun's covered stock jutting forward from beneath the man's left leg.

Phillipe Beneteau had reinserted the eagle feather in his hat band at the same moment he had paused outside of Deadwood to exchange his boots for the comfort of moccasins. With the feather and beaded footwear in place, he felt free to travel among the Indian tribes, but without them, he was a white man.

Feather out and boots on, he could mingle with the white men and not be called "half–breed," never be kicked out of the bars, allowed inside their churches, even though he wasn't a church-going man.

He reasoned as he rode that it wasn't his fault the man's wife decided to share a drink with him at the Deadwood bar. Nor did he think she was worth fighting for when her husband called him outside after making her marital status known. The gun business was the husband's idea and Phillipe Beneteau had outdrawn him fair and square. It seemed a good idea, however, to move on lest his friends got carried away that a stranger had wounded one of their own.

The piebald's ears perked; Buster chattered in alarm.

Beneteau's bronzed right hand slid over the black-handled six-gun, but he kept the horse moving at the same steady pace. The animal's ears riveted on a butte where a group of man-sized columns of gumbo stood eroding in sagebrush. He glared at the edges of the clay spires for movement.

The horse slid on its haunches and reared nearly unseating both Beneteau and the raccoon when four nearby sagebrush plants toppled. Beneteau leapt to the ground, reins in one hand and handgun whipped from its holster by the other.

Four Indians stood up, their dark eyes watching him without any show of emotion. Two held bows, one a flintlock and the other a shotgun.

"Hinhanska, we did not know it was you," said one of the warriors, signing with his arms for the others to lower their weapons. The Indians' bodies were dulled by sand, they wore no feathers and had no paint on their faces. The leader had called Beneteau by his Indian name in Sioux.

“Kicking Hawk, you have set your trap for a prairie chicken and caught only a White Owl,” Beneteau said, relaxing and accepting the name by which the Sioux called him.

“You looked like a wasichun. We thought you were an illegal trapper. The white–head soldier has given us permission to protect our land from them. But only one man rides with a living death mask behind him.”

“I have been south of Deadwood and now go to my people in the Turtle Mountains. They prepare for the spring buffalo hunt.”

“The Métis are our cousins. We trade with you and share the buffalo. Would that all white people had the blood of Chippewa and Yanktonai mixed with the white breeds. There would be less warfare, Hinhanska.”

The four Indians led Beneteau to the gully in which they had tied their ponies. They squatted to talk, after Beneteau went to his saddlebags and withdrew a twist of tobacco he gave to the friendly Sioux.

“Thank you, Hinhanska,” Kicking Hawk said. He removed his red clay pipe from a beaded, rawhide pouch and filled the bowl with flakes he shaved from the new tobacco. They sat cross–legged in a circle and passed the pipe sunwise when it was lit.

“The white men are driving large herds of long–horned cattle north,” Beneteau said. “The prairie grass is short again this year.”

“We have heard they are coming,” Kicking Hawk replied. “We have also heard they only give Indians a few animals to eat.”

"They have a word in their language you don't have," Beneteau said. "It is 'own'."

"Ah-oan," said Kicking Hawk. The other three braves sat hunched, quiet. One tried the new word and they laughed. "What does it mean?" said Kicking Hawk.

Beneteau said it meant that the weapons they had belonged only to them.

They "owned" them. The Indians shrugged and smiled at the foolishness of not being able to share each others weapons.

"Do you ah-oan the tobacco you brought, Hinhanska? Do you ah-oan Mother Earth whose breast pushed the plant forth for Grandfather Sun to grow?"

"No, Kicking Hawk. But it is the white man's way and I understand it."

"Here, Hinhanska. Take my pipe. Now you ah-oan it."

Beneteau knew the size of the honor. He undid his holster and its belt of fourty-four cartridges and wrapped it around the Colt. He thrust it forward to Kicking Hawk.

The Indian's eyes narrowed into thin slits and he stared hard into the White Owl's face to detect a twitch of remorse. Kicking Hawk saw none, and he shook off the gift.

"You have a long way to travel and not all those you meet will be your friends. Keep the gun, Hinhanska. When we meet again, you will think good of your brothers, the Yanktonai."

Buster jabbered. One of the warriors, who had crawled above the gully for a look, slid back among them, his legs and buckskin–covered backside rasping on the clay in the stillness. He spoke quietly to Kicking Hawk, motioning toward the south with his arm.

"He says there are men riding fast this way," Kicking Hawk said.

"That could be a posse," said Beneteau.

"Are these men after you?"

"It'd be a little hard to explain. There was a woman in Deadwood at the bar. I didn't know she was married until her husband walked in."

"He ah–oan her, Hinhanska?"

"Something like that, old friend. We had a fight and bullets flew. I didn't stick around. He must have died."

"Come, Hinhanska, we will show you a way out."

The five men, one with the raccoon riding double, mounted and spurred their horses to a gallop along the dry creek bed.

The escape could have worked, but it hadn't snowed or rained in a month. Dust from their horses rose like a fog behind them, the cloud a telling sign to those on higher ground.

By the time Beneteau and the Indians broke from the creek bed across a flat stretch leading into the hills, the men had cut across toward the dust.

Beneteau held the rangy piebald in, and Kicking Hawk looked over at him and smiled. The raccoon clung behind its tall man friend, its bushy shape bobbing smooth with the gait of the horse. Without a word, the Indian leader broke away, leading the other three braves toward a stretch of rough gumbo hills into which they disappeared.

Beneteau released his hold on the reins and the big horse lengthened its stride. The posse ignored the Indians and headed after the single rider.

Beneteau admired the piebald. The gap widened their lead. He felt the big animal's legs soar off the ground to clear a washout that blocked their escape. The dark gap blurred below them before the horse slammed back onto solid ground. The impact unseated the raccoon, which hit the ground in a puff of dust exploding around it, then rolled in a ball and came up chattering but back on its four paws.

Beneteau reined the horse and whirled. He touched the animal's ribs lightly with his heels and swept toward the band of men pursuing him. They could not see the small animal below the level of the sagebrush. The posse's momentum faltered as the men braced for the fugitive's charge.

Beneteau swooped low from the saddle as he and the horse shot past Buster. The coon reached up to the man's outstretched hand and was back behind the saddle. They turned and the chase renewed, but the distance between Beneteau and his pursuers had shrunk.

"Damn it, Buster, you could get us both killed," Beneteau yelled in the onrushing wind.

Looking back at the posse, Beneteau saw rifles dancing like dark sticks in the hands of some of the men. The air whined over and around him as bullets smashed through it before he heard the muffled pop of the shots. He felt like a coyote with a pack of mad dogs after him. Beneteau zig–zagged the piebald to distort the shooters' aim, at the same time undoing the flap over the Henry. On his second turn, the rifle was in his hands, the reins in his clenched teeth. Riding oblique to the posse, he leveled the rifle and squeezed off the first round. The bullet he fired kicked up dust in front of the lead rider. The shot was low, and Beneteau leaned his horse into a turn left. The second bullet caught the pursuing rider in the right shoulder, the slug's impact tearing the man from his saddle. The posse men reined up and grouped around their fallen comrade.

Beneteau slid the black to its haunches and emptied the rifle at his pursuers while they struggled to raise the wounded man. He rammed the Henry back in its home and spurred his horse on a straight course again. They galloped through a break in the hills and dropped down into brown buttes which were thinly timbered. When they got to the Cannonball River, Beneteau knew the posse had fallen back.

He held the horse from drinking and sought a spot to make camp. The animal would get water after it cooled. Buster rode one-handed, the free one rubbing dust from its nose. The raccoon's fur was ruffled from the tumble it had taken and from the wind during the wild ride. Beneteau reached in his shirt pocket and withdrew a pinch of pemmican. He pushed the meat under Buster's nose, and the raccoon snatched the morsel with its free paw. The man took another pinch, which he ate himself. The dried buffalo, ground corn and berries soaked in bone marrow refreshed his body with new energy. The raccoon tugged on his shirt for more.

"Sorry, pardner, this isn't a feast. Keep your eyes open for a camping place." The coon sensed the tone of his voice and settled back to the tempo of the horse. The man figured if the posse came on, they'd be looking for him at sheltered spots near water. He rode toward a small lump on the grey and brown prairie and was pleased by a chalky bare spot at its base where rain had eroded a small washout. It was big enough to hide in while they rested. Buster jumped to his shoulder when he dismounted. The coon scurried down the man's side and rolled in the dirt. The creature fluffed its fur while the man loosened the saddle cinch and slipped the bit from the horse's mouth. Beneteau took a small, pegged rawhide rope from his saddlebag with one hand and dipped a handful of grain from the bag with the other. He rubbed the animal's nose and gave it the grain before snubbing its halter to the rawhide rope and driving the peg in the ground with a rock. The coon chattered and picked through the kernels which fell from the horse's mouth. Beneteau scouted the countryside around the depression, saw nothing and laid down to nap. The coon curled up beside his warm body.

The sun had set when he awoke. Stars were breaking through the blackness above. It was a clear night and silent without wind. His chest and arm felt warm where Buster was curled, but the animal sensed him stir and sat up, too. The man crawled out of the washout for a look and saw nothing. He heard only the wail of coyotes. He shared another pinch of pemmican with the raccoon.

"Let's go, pardner, we've got to get Bronc some water and keep moving." The coon's rapid jabber signaled its pleasure. They mounted and headed back to the river.

Beneteau heard the water gurgle over a beaver dam when they approached. His tenseness spread to Buster, who sat erect, ears pointed at each new noise around them. Beneteau stepped off the horse but pushed the coon back on the saddle while the big animal drank.

"Wait your turn," he whispered firmly. He took the bit from the piebald's mouth so it could drink freely, then got his canteen from the other saddlebag. The canteen's canvas-covered metal side thumped hollowly in the dark when it bumped the riverbank. The canteen gurgled half-full of river water when Beneteau flinched at the first splash of water against his face after the flash in brush from upstream. The rifle report followed and more shots exploded around him. He rolled, dropping the canteen, and he tried to control the frightened horse. Bronc's head slipped from the loose bridle, and he galloped off with the raccoon chattering wildly from his perch on the saddle. Beneteau, bridle and reins in one hand, the Colt in the other scrambled for cover. He dipped behind a cut in the riverbank. He counted at least five positions from which firing was coming, but he didn't return fire.

"I think we got the son of a bitch," he heard a man shout.

"Can you see him?"

"Nah, but he ain't moving."

"Let the bastard have it again."

The shooting started up off to Beneteau's left in the direction where the canteen had clattered into the river. He took advantage of the noise to crawl up the bank and steal away in the darkness. He could hear Buster somewhere ahead, and he hoped the raccoon was still in the saddle. The dim outline of the horse reassured him. Bronc stood waiting, and he slipped the bridle back on and rolled up on the horse's back, his right leg passing smoothly over the crouched form of the coon.

"Let's get the hell out of here," he mumbled, and the piebald broke into a gallop. He and Buster didn't get a drink. The posse must have split itself, or he was sure he would have been filled full of holes at the river. "Hang on, Buster. The Heart River's ahead of us somewhere."

He let Bronc set the pace, and the horse slowed to a trot. At times, the man and the coon tensed, clinging one to the saddle horn the other to the man's shirt when the horse nosed into a ravine. Beneteau hoped his horse would keep its footing. The horse loped after sliding down a bank, then slowed to a trot again as the ground leveled.

As they rode northerly, Beneteau's mind wandered back to the bar. Father Belgarde had warned him and his little friends of the evil of drinking and bad women who liked such men. The priest would come to the Métis log homes in the Turtles and gather the children to bring them to the one-room, church cabin the older men had built for him. The priest taught them to say "Salud Marie" on the Rosary. Beneteau thought he still didn't know what Father Belgarde was talking about when he said God would give him grace if he prayed. You couldn't eat grace, couldn't shoot it. The older men might have called it luck. Good luck if you hit what you shot, bad luck if you missed a charging buffalo and your horse stumbled. Was that what Father Belgarde meant? God gave you good luck and bad. The priest taught the commandments. "Thou shalt not commit adultery." But the older men weren't above responding to a wink from any woman, be she married or unmarried. Only women who wore bandannas and kept their eyes down were left alone. How could you avoid the others? They made you feel wanted, needed. That woman back in the Deadwood bar. She didn't have to be in there. She was there looking, and she saw him and wanted him. He merely responded. He was sharing a drink with her when her husband came in and started shouting at them. Maybe, if the man had not struck his wife in the face. Maybe, Phillipe Beneteau would have got up and moved away and accepted the insults.

He longed to see Maria, dark-haired, dark-eyed, a bright white smile and slim, long legs. She had fire in her. She could ride and shoot, and you didn't feel burdened by her. She could take care of herself, yet be soft and gentle. She was one of the few women riders he wouldn't mind on the spring buffalo hunt. She could be mysterious, as well, but when her mind was on the business of hunting buffalo, that side of her nature came out strong. Damn, that woman could ride and shoot straight.

Beneteau had been far enough south to see a dozen Texas cowboys moving 5,000 head of long–horn steers northward. He watched them from a lookout butte, studied their method and marveled at the control they exercised over the beasts. Buffalo went where they wanted. Buffalo were exciting. That's why he was eager to return home. The carts were being repaired and put in shape right now even as he rode in the darkness. Métis men were making trips to Devils Lake to have their buffalo guns fixed by Cousin Lamaroux. Lamaroux's French father had been a gun smith, his mother full–blooded Chippewa. He had taken the white man's path but didn't forget his roots in the Turtles. The settlers Beneteau saw were a sorry lot. They spoke a dozen foreign tongues, feared the Indians and just seemed to want to travel on the road to anything that was dull. When he saw the cowboys gather around their only wagon one evening, all but four rode off toward a little town they were passing. He followed and heard their six–guns roar when they rode down the main street. They tethered their mounts at the saloon hitching post, and Beneteau heard the music and laughter bubble from the weather–beaten building. Most any of them would have made buffalo hunters. They might even have preferred it to the boredom of following behind the long–horns.

Still, the cowboys and cattle were coming north. The prairie was an expansive grassland, but Phillipe Beneteau could smell a change brewing. The older men worried every year that the buffalo were disappearing. Their long–standing friendship with the tribes was under strain. The Métis could hunt, ride and think with the best. It was the mixed blessing from God the Great Spirit. At times Beneteau's own blood ran hot from his Indian side. And he also felt on occasion an urge to walk into a building and act civilized. Was not the Métis leader Louis Riel cultured? Never mind all that complicated stuff. He just wanted to see Maria again and go on the hunt.

The piebald nickered and Beneteau felt a slight trace of moisture in the air. His throat was dry, and Buster had been quiet for a long time but now perked up. The Heart River slithered in front of them somewhere, and they looked forward to a drink.

The sun broke through the dark and spread pink on the horizon as wind kicked up. Beneteau dropped off the horse, and Buster jumped from his shoulder to the ground. The man cupped his hands and drank from the river. The coon lapped at the water and began to wash itself. Beneteau let the horse drink again. The night air had kept him cool, and the pace was not forced. When they had their fill, he tethered the horse, took his rifle and followed the stream against the rising wind. Three deer ignored him for an instant when he slipped around a river bend. He singled out a young buck and it fell behind the report of his shot, a split second before the other two vanished. Beneteau slit the animal's throat and gutted it, carefully removing the paunch, which he dumped on the ground, then washed in the river. He didn't like to waste meat, but cut away only the hindquarters and lugged them on his neck back to his horse and the raccoon. Beneteau filled the paunch with water and tied it at the top with a strand of deer tendon. He tucked a strip of the deer's back hide under the center of the hindquarters and lashed it above his bedroll. The sun was brightening the grey dawn when he got back on the piebald, and they moved from the river back into the open hill country. Beneteau's eyes ranged in a wide circle, but little was moving except the air currents, which were ebbing and flowing with increasing intensity. The wind was annoying, and he headed the horse for a clump of brush in a gully well away from the river. It felt good to slip into the lee of the hillside where he dismounted and hid the horse in a patch of bare chokecherry bushes. He got a small fire going, cut a pair of willow limbs which he shaved to points on each end. He drove the sticks into the ground near the fire and propped them at a slant with rocks, then hung venison on the open tips. He handed Buster a chunk of the raw, red meat and the coon turned it over and over, nibbling it carefully. The cooked venison warmed Beneteau inside. He placed a round, granite rock in the fire, then gouged in the earth a clay–lined bowl, which he filled with water. The rock hissed when he put it in the depression, he then rolled it back out with a stick. He sprinkled a handful of dried mint leaves over the water, then filled a tin cup with the tea before he settled back for a smoke. He made a cigarette and watched it shorten itself with each draw he took. Buster came over and fiddled with the shiny fourty-four's in his cartridge belt. Beneteau ignored the animal to doze away exhaustion.

Before his eyes opened, Beneteau knew something was not right. He felt the cold steel pressed against his cheekbone.

"You could have run to the North Pole, you son of a bitch. We'd have got ya," said the man who held the rifle barrel to his face.

Phillipe Beneteau's hand touched his empty holster.

"What's your name, breed?" a second member of the posse said, snarling at him.

A man who held the piebald spit tobacco juice on the ground. "What the hell difference does it make what his name is? Get him up on this horse. There's a cottonwood limb waiting to help wring his worthless neck." Two of the men forced Beneteau to his feet and bound his hands behind him before pushing him up on the horse's back.

Phillipe Beneteau said nothing. The absence of Buster stuck in his mind, but there was no use struggling. The posse men had him outnumbered, and he just felt empty at the thought that his luck had run out.

"You sure had us fooled," said the man who had pushed the rifle against his face. "We had trouble figurin' you out. Thought you was a white man. Once we saw the remains of that deer with its stomach gone, we just started thinkin' Indian. No sense in us ridin' main trails once we figured you was a half-breed."

"To hell with that crap, Cal. Let's hang his worthless ass and get back home."

The six riders moved out of the sheltered spot and rode toward a dip in the horizon from which a dark outline showed a clump of trees growing.

Chapter 2

Phillipe Beneteau went Indian in his mind. His hazel eyes hardened into a sightless glaze. His handsome features betrayed no emotion. He was as the whites would say, stoic. But beneath his outward indifference, he was as taut as a bowstring. The posse mens' voices rasped on his brain cells deep within his mind. He heard the hoof steps of their horses. Honest sweat from the lathered horses mixed its fragrance with the sweetness of sage and flowed with the early morning air into his nostrils. These were the odors of freedom to roam over Mother Earth beholden to no man except self. Yet, self had betrayed him, allowed him to be taken. He rode ready to die, determined to live.

"Hey, breed," one of the riders said. "Didn't your squaw ever tell you your kind aren't allowed in a white man's saloon?" The rider slammed the butt of his rifle into Beneteau's ribs.

Beneteau didn't answer, didn't wince or groan. Pain bowed to self's gloom as he rode his last ride.

"There's a nice clump of cottonwoods below that bank, Cal," one of the men said, motioning to what had been the dark speck before them. The riders approached the Heart River near where Beneteau had killed the deer.

"They do not need me like I needed you, brother," Beneteau thought about the deer, who, too, had lost its life this day but not its spirit. He envied the two deer that had fled to freedom, and he knew that chance, not choice, was a big part of life. Buster had gotten away. The little animal could return to life along the creek if it could stay out of the white man's traps.

The riders dismounted and tied their horses when they got to the trees.

"You can just sit up there pretty as a picture," said the man who hit him with the rifle. "You won't have long to wait for the necktie party."

The posse men built a fire and got a pot of coffee brewing in a chipped, blue enameled vessel, blackened to the lips. They untied the venison strapped behind Beneteau's saddle, cut strips and hung them to roast. The meat hissed back at the fire before it released its aroma into the air.

"He looks like a white man, don't he?" a thickset man said from a crouched position. "You sure we won't get our asses in a sling for lynching his no good hide?"

"He's a breed all right," said the nasty one. "He smells like an Indian."

"I wouldn't have been sure," the man called Cal said. "There's a few white renegades riding around wearing moccasins and feathers and hanging out with Indians. But when he cut out that deer paunch from those entrails. Ain't no white man would do that. He's a breed, all right."

"He's as good as dead," the nasty one said. "We sure enjoy your vittles. What's your name, breed? Hate to take a man's food and not thank him." His brown–stained teeth showed behind a grunting laugh.

"Go easy on him, Blackie." another of the posse men said. "He won't be around long and maybe he needs some time to think about his sins."

"Yeh, lookee there. I think he's got a cross around his neck. You got religion, breed?" The man called Blackie walked to where Beneteau sat silently staring straight ahead. The man reached up and tugged sharply on the crude wooden cross that had flopped over Beneteau's grey, wool shirt front. The thong bit sharply into the back of Beneteau's neck before it snapped.

"You'd a thought even a breed would have got enough religion to know to leave a man's wife alone," said Blackie, glaring darkly at the cross. Then, gunning Cal's brother down in cold blood. "You're a dead man."

Beneteau remained stoic but felt the pain inside. The cross from Father Belgarde was given when he had received his First Communion in the Turtle Mountains. He wore it as a necklace and told Indians it was his "medicine." Just like their eagle claws and bird beaks. Instead of tucking it in a medicine bundle, he wore it hidden beneath his tunic. White people wore the Christian symbol around the neck, and he had their blood, too.

The word religion slipped into the maze of his thoughts. The priest had told the little children they could pray and be good and God would reward them in the next life. Beneteau thought it was now that he could use some help. When he tried to pray the way the priest taught, he had always done it with great hope, then felt empty when his prayers were not answered. He had prayed at ten for a gun to hunt rabbits, and no angel had brought one. He could pray now. But if the Great Spirit didn't understand his predicament, it seemed no amount of praying was going to open His eyes. Beneteau remembered the first gun he finally got at age fourteen. He had run a trap line through the winter to catch mink and fox. Once a snowshoe rabbit hit his snare on a cold, still night as he followed his trap line trail through the snow under bright moonlight. The animal wailed its eerie death song sharply through the woods. From those animal pelts stretched carefully on drying boards, he got the money to buy the small-bore gun in spring at the trader's store. It was used, the stock dried and scarred, cast off by a settler who found its 25.20 caliber too small for buffalo and bear. With a half-box of shells, he marched home to Koohkoum Emma's cabin. "*A bien!*" she said, smiling proudly, when he held up the rifle. "*You are now a man, Nooshishim.*"

He lived with her since his Chippewa–Cree mother and French–Métis father had made a trip north to visit relatives in Canada and never returned. He and grandma used to talk by the stone fireplace grandpa had built before he died of the coughing. "*Maybe the wolves ate them,*" grandma would say about his folks. But Beneteau even then understood that his father was wanted by authorities in St. Paul, and he would not be back. Maybe he had killed some man, too. The other men talked about it, but went silent when the young son approached. He could tell by their empty looks he was on his own. Koohkoum kept him, fed him, tried to make him walk the straight path but never scolded. She was the one woman he could truly say he loved. She made a fine rabbit stew. But the rifle, it had not come from an angel. And Beneteau did not expect an angel to appear now to untie his hands and lead Bronc to the high ground to show his speed to this posse gang again.

"Hey, breed. We'd share this with you, but where you're goin', you won't be hungry. Plenty warm, but I never heard of anyone bein' hungry in hell," said Blackie.

Beneteau etched the man's features in his mind. His black cowboy hat brim hung limply over enlarged ears. His beard was almost charcoal black, his eyes; cold blue and mean. A button nose popped from the hair on his face, and a half-moon scar traced a path from near the right nostril around the side of his eye and finished its arch on his forehead. He may have been kicked in the face by a horse. Beneteau hoped so. He would show these enemies no emotion, but this man brought up a white–hot hatred inside his guts. This one was the kind who would stay in his mind until breath left his body. The man enjoyed seeing him suffer. His dangling to stillness at the end of a rope would give the man pleasure. It was an unbearable thought.

Beneteau cut off a groan of anguish that gurgled into his throat. He watched the men break off from their meal and slip away to relieve themselves.

Bronc's head was snubbed by the rawhide halter thong to a slim cottonwood. Beneteau's hands were tied together and lashed to the saddle horn.

The halter thong was tied under the knot with only two strands of leather. It was a break knot to enable the horse to pull free from a brush fire touched off by a camp fire. Bronc never ran far when loose. He loved a handful of grain and that kept him close to Beneteau no matter the danger. The posse men straggled out and back to their campfire. The man called Cal huddled by it with his back toward the captive. Beneteau dug his moccasins deep into the piebald's ribs and the startled horse lunged. The thong snapped it's halter end and slapped back against the horse's nose. Bronc reared, came down at a hard slant away from the tree, and the man and horse were off and running at full gait away from the posse men.

"Shoot that bastard," Beneteau heard yelled behind him. He and Bronc lunged up a creek bank and broke out of sight of his captors. By the time the posse appeared behind, they were out in front 250 yards, Beneteau bent low over his mount's neck, guiding the racing buffalo runner with his knees. He was free again. By chance, headed back toward the chokecherry bushes where he had been captured. As the big horse warmed to his run, Beneteau thought of the trail that led through the brush and between the hillsides that flanked the spot. He urged Bronc. The horse strained. The lead widened. Beneteau heard scattered shots behind him. The posse had been caught off guard.

Ahead, Beneteau saw a masked fur ball at the edge of the opening to the thicket of berry bushes. Buster waited for him. Beneteau forced the toes of his moccasins against Bronc's shoulders, and the horse slowed.

"*Nakee*!" Beneteau ordered. The piebald slid to a halt.

Beneteau nudged him to a tree. The raccoon, chattering wildly, rattled up the trunk and plopped on its riding spot behind the man, who turned the horse with his knees and set it into a full gallop again along the trail. They drove down the incline, dust churning behind them, and onto the grey–brown, rolling prairie hills. From here on, the posse didn't have a chance in hell of catching them again. Bronc could run all day and like it. Beneteau had first seen the horse as a colt cavorting with a band of Sioux ponies and traded his old .32 caliber Winchester for it. Bronc was the best buffalo runner the Métis ever had. His tribesmen didn't call Beneteau, *"D'or Métis," the Golden Métis*, just because of his looks. He had, they said, a *golden* way with horses and guns.

When he looked back, Beneteau saw the five–man posse pull up to watch their quarry flee. They had his Colt and cross but had left the Henry rest in its scabbard. The thongs binding his hands to the saddle horn ripped into his wrists and stained them crimson. Only now did he feel the pain sear his mind. He was free, but not free. Beneteau's mind slipped back to the memory of the coyote foot he had found in one of his traps. The coyote was in the wide–open space of the Creator's world but trapped and left to die by man. The dog of the Great Spirit chewed its leg through the bone and escaped. He took the foot home and put it in a small cedar box he had pegged together with slim willow sticks. He vowed never to take another animal's life unless his own depended on it and then, only with a fervent plea for forgiveness. That was the Indian way—use the world but with reverence and thanksgiving.

They topped a ridge and dropped into the shelter of a cut bank where they stopped. Whether the posse came on or not, he must free his hands. The pain built, and he was losing blood.

Buster clamored for attention. The animal slipped around Beneteau's midsection and ran its paws up his shirt front. The coon stood on its rear legs and pressed its cold nose against the man's face, then gently nibbled his nose.

Beneteau's eyes winced as he tried to withdraw his face from the affectionate animal.

"You've got to give me a hand, pardner. I can't even get off this horse with my hands tied. Come, Buster, give it a try."

The coon backed down from its embrace, turned and brushed its fluffy tail into Beneteau's face, then came about to search for treats.

"Buster," the man said firmly, "*noo.*"

The coon trilled, then sat back puzzled by the rebuff. Its nose caught the scent of blood, and he eyed the man's bound hands. The animal nuzzled Beneteau's wrists and lapped the rawhide which was soaked red. Its front paws fondled the strip of hide. The animal was hungry and began to nibble at what tasted like fresh meat. Beneteau talked softly to the critter, encouraged it, cautioned the little animal when its teeth slipped from the hide and grated against his burning wrists.

The task was agonizingly slow. The coon paused to wash its paws, then turn its eyes to the man's face to seek approval. The coon sensed tension and was puzzled. The man friend did nothing except use his voice.

"Do it, little friend. Have another bite. Get at it, Buster."

The coon's sharp teeth cut through the leather and Beneteau wriggled loose. With hands hanging limp in pain, he gathered the little critter in his forearms and drew it toward him. The animal licked his face and grunted under the embrace. Beneteau dismounted and withdrew a handful of ground comfrey leaves from his saddlebag. He sprinkled the powder on one wrist, then the other and the blood clotted. His French father had taught him the healing value of the herb. They were back in the saddle, and Beneteau pushed the piebald to a ground–gobbling lope. The coon clung to his shirt and trilled.

Earlier in the day, they needed meat and water, now they needed both again, but Beneteau felt naked without his Colt and medicine cross.

His mind see–sawed. He should keep going. He was free. As long as a man had a gun, he could make a living on the prairie, and he could keep his own counsel. Sure his friends always admired the ebony–handled fourty–four. It had balance and fit into his hand like it was family. But Phillipe Beneteau knew that the Henry was his tool of the trade as buffalo hunter. He had it, so let the other go. Let it be. Women came and went in his life and like them he had had other guns. *Don't be foolish about the Colt.* He fought against the other thought, the empty spot where the cross rested on his chest. He felt reassured by touching it with his hand. Once, when he bathed in Willow Creek, he dressed quickly and rode back deep into the Turtle Mountains before he realized in a panic moment that he was not wearing his medicine cross. It was important to him. He felt the Great Spirit, the God Father Belgarde talked about, would not ride with him if he didn't wear his sign. A man who was at odds with God on the lonely prairie could be warmed only outside by a campfire, never inside where his own hungry spirit was. This empty spot at his neck bothered him the most. With the cross in place, he could ride through the Maker's thunderstorms without seeking shelter. He had done it, confident that God would not strike down one of his followers. Though thunder boasted loud and lightning struck near, Phillipe Beneteau could smile in a pelting rain and keep riding for he knew God was with him because of the cross. He turned back. He rode back to get the missing medicine cross at Willow Creek. He must now circle the posse and try to pick up their trail to get it back again. The posse men were far enough away from Deadwood to have to make camp for the night.

A jackrabbit skipped out of a nearby chunk of bunch grass. Beneteau whistled through his teeth and the rabbit bounced to a stop and stood frozen. The Henry recoiled against his shoulder, and the jackrabbit dropped a split second after the report. Buster was on the ground pulling on the rabbit's long ears before Beneteau had time to dismount. The coon was excited at the other animal's stillness. They found a depression out of the wind, and Beneteau gouged a hole for a fire. He dressed the animal, and hung its dangling carcass from two strips of rawhide tied to its long ears. Two small rock piles held the free ends of the rawhide, and Beneteau poked the carcass into a gentle rock as it cooked above the flames. He fed the fire from a small pile of sticks he and Buster gathered, and he sliced meat from the rabbit as it cooked. The coon rolled a chunk of meat in its paws and nibbled it.

The meat renewed Beneteau's spirits but did nothing for his throbbing wrists. The bleeding had stopped. Beneteau crawled from the depression and looked around, but nothing moved as far as he could see, so he crawled back. He and Buster snuggled together while they napped.

Beneteau's eyes drifted fitfully in and out of sleep. Several times he awoke with a start, crawled out of the low spot for a look, then slithered back for a few more moments of rest.

It was late afternoon, the sun beginning to stretch the long shadows of the hills to the east when he got up and went to give a handful of grain to the piebald. He dusted his wrists with comfrey powder again and licked his parched lips. Life got miserable in a hurry without water. Buster didn't seem to mind anything. The coon wobbled around, eying the man, waiting for him to make his move up over the horse and drop his foot so the little animal could climb to the cantle. The creature loved to ride horseback.

"We better find us a water hole," Beneteau said softly as they moved out into the open. Again, the man had taken the slain critter's stomach lining for a makeshift canteen.

Beneteau stayed wide to the east of the trail the posse had followed. The sun was almost up when they came to a slough with pockets of water oozing from small bowls in the earth. They stopped to drink. Beneteau watched a great horned owl rise softly from the high slough grass, a small rodent trailing an intestine clutched firmly in its strong talons. The owl floated to a nearby rock outcrop on a small hill and sat staring at them with big yellow eyes, pausing to rip from its prey a beakful of red meat. That the owl stayed near was comforting to Beneteau. That it was busy eating and did not hoot was like a blessing from above. He was chilled by the hooting of any owl, although he could not say with certainty that it was always bad luck. Whenever he did hear an owl and bad luck followed, he remembered it clearly though. Koohkoum had taught him about owls. So he was happy this one was busy devouring its meal.

They drank deeply from the spring–fed hole. The piebald's soft mouth dripped water and it flung its head back. The raccoon's nose looked pointed where the water had matted its fur flat against its mouth. Beneteau took the Sacred Pipe and a sack of tobacco from one side of his saddlebag. He filled it and sat down to smoke. He looked at the red pipestone, a single feather dangling from its stem. He lit the tobacco and drew in deeply before releasing the mouthful of smoke into the air. It was a sacred moment as he sent his thoughts to God with the smoke currents. He also enjoyed the taste of the tobacco smoke rippling inside him. He was thankful to be alive.

He began to think of his predicament. He was on his way home to the Turtles to report on the cattle herd coming and to prepare with his people for the buffalo hunt. The hunts he had grown up with were ranging further west. Long ago, the Métis would load their carts and herd their horses to Devils Lake. They had only to worry about the Sioux, whose objections the hunters overcame by trading them old muskets and copper pots for furs. The Sioux respected the Métis as fighters, and many were related through intermarriage. The Indians could understand that trade with Métis brought them better guns, and their women were fond of the colored blankets, pots, and beads. Yes, the buffalo were moving further west, but they were still out there. Unlike white hunters, the Métis could parley with the tribes. The Métis had no desire to dominate the Indians, to destroy forever the hunting grounds. Some of his people farmed, but only small parcels in the mountains. But the whites wanted to change everything. Beneteau thought he understood some of it. Some of the Métis had been East, even to Europe. They brought back stories of hordes of people and huge stone buildings. There was no room to roam in either place. Barons and counts and rich people controlled the land.

Talk in the winter of 1882-83 was about rumors of white men bringing in domestic cattle in great droves. Rumors were always bigger than life, and the elders had picked Phillipe Beneteau to ride south to learn if there was truth to the claims. They joked that he could ride among whites and not be noticed. And so he had set out until he had come to the herd of long-horned cattle he met coming north. The bar business? Maybe, if he had stood his ground, it would have been all right. The husband of the woman had no right to take such offense at the wayward actions of his wife. Beneteau knew in his heart, however, that if it became known he was a breed, he was in trouble. It was impossible, for him to control his red blood that told him to flee, rather than run the risk of the white man's justice. He just tasted it. He heard the worry by one of the posse men that they might be hanging a white man.

But a breed. Hang him. No one would care. Still, Phillipe Beneteau could take the feather from his hat and put his boots back on and walk among the white man without fear that his looks would betray him. Being half red made it hard to understand the white ways at times, but the same was true of the white side of his nature. Red men were more tolerant of their half brothers, the Métis, but inwardly there was a cultural chasm neither seemed fully able to bridge. Odd, that males of the races thought they were superior to the others.

Beneteau put the Sacred Pipe back in the saddlebag with the feather from his hat and the rabbit–skin canteen. He got his boots out of the other bag and stored his moccasins in their place. Now he would be white again for a spell. He cinched the saddle tight and slipped on Bronc's back and the raccoon sat behind him, happy again to be moving. They headed south.

Chapter 3

Beneteau had ridden long and hard to get to the Breasts of Mother Earth, two round–topped buttes that jutted skyward above an old spring–laced Indian campground. If he guessed right, the posse would abandon the open country he had taken them through in favor of following a known trail on their return to Deadwood.

He could gaze out on that trail and spot them coming almost as soon as they could see where he lie hidden on the towering landmarks ahead of them.

His water supply was low, but Beneteau chose to climb the lower of the two buttes on its east side rather than leave tracks at the springs. He tied Bronc in a clump of brush and picked a path to the flat above. He peered over its edge, covered by an old rock cairn. A short pathway of sandstone led to the cairn. He could lie and wait in the cairn, worn from the wind that beat against the hilltop. Buster wandered among the rocks, pawing them and picking up black beetles which the animal crushed in its teeth before spitting out the bugs' hard shells.

The raccoon kept busy exploring, munching on something, but the man and animal had a bond between them that signaled quiet when the man grew still and tense. The raccoon would flatten and stop chattering and eye the man and if he ordered, *"Ayaw!"* the coon went dormant until released from the command. For now, the man was content to let the animal ramble. The coon watched the man friend doctor his wrists. His wool shirt had been rolled back at the sleeves. The wrists were stained green from the comfrey powder and tingled under the herb's healing power.

Beneteau wondered how best he could make an approach to the campsite at the springs. He wanted to make his move in the dark. Unlike Buster, Beneteau knew he, too, was more vulnerable at night. So he would study the area before assaulting the camp, then let Bronc have his head when they retreated and trust that the horse would follow a safe path. If his plan worked, the posse men would not even know they had been visited until morning, and he would be well on his way north again. This time, surprise was on his side. The posse would not be looking for him. They might be alert for an attack from a band of marauding Indians, but white men seemed to think they were safer at night once they had a campfire going. Métis would use the advantage of darkness.

While they waited, Beneteau and Buster played their game of hide and seek. The man tossed a stone into the grass. The coon waddled in the direction of the tossed object, sniffed the air, circled sniffing some more, then ambled toward it. Beneteau admired the little critter's sense of smell. Its black paws groped in front of it, frantically fondling the grass until it picked up the stone Beneteau had thrown. The animal retrieved the stone for a treat of the dried meat the man friend carried in his shirt pocket. The coon associated the scent of this man with pleasure. Knowing its fondness for trinkets, Beneteau tossed both a stone and a rifle cartridge he had rubbed in his hands. The raccoon found the stone, but when its nose caught the other scent, it also picked up the shiny cartridge and returned both for its expected treat.

Beneteau ruffled the fur on the animal's head, and the coon gnawed the tips of his fingers playfully. They and Bronc were about as close as a man and animals get.

Beneteau saw a circle of soaring turkey buzzards. Ahead and below of their gliding turns, he detected movement. He watched the ground shapes become more distinct until he identified them as riders, probably white men, who had a tendency to ride abreast of each other, despite the narrowness of a trail which had been used for years for efficiency of passage.

Rather than risk discovery, he and Buster headed back down the slope to Bronc, who snorted at their approach.

The man and coon mounted the horse and rode further down the slope to follow a drainage a mile away from the butte top where they stopped. They waited for the sun to go down. At dusk, they moved back up the drainage and Beneteau guided the horse part way up the hill on the southern side. They were halfway to his lookout when Beneteau dismounted and led the horse. The coon, having sensed the man's taut manner, had grown still in the saddle. The animal's dark eyes glistened.

Beneteau saw the campfire flames dance through the bunch grass and fade into blackness surrounding the spring pothole. He needed to identify the riders.

He retraced his path across the butte's midsection until he reached his former point of ascent. He urged Bronc back down, and they circled in the dark until they touched the trail coming out of the south side of the spring. Beneteau let the horse have his head to follow the path at a walk. It was worn and silent. The campfire glowed against airborne dust particles above where the riders camped. Beneteau angled from the trail until he came to a patch of brush. He tied Bronc with the reins, left the cinch tight on the saddle and stroked the horse's neck before setting forth on foot. Buster tagged along with him and Beneteau didn't mind. The coon's night vision was better than his own.

If the coon sensed danger from other animals or snakes in their path it could trill an alarm that would be just another natural noise in the night.

When they were within earshot of the men's voices, Beneteau dropped to his belly and crawled forward toward a clump of swamp grass that formed a silhouette to hide him.

Beneteau was pleased when he saw the floppy, black hat worn by Blackie draw back from where he sat tossing sticks on the fire. Shadows danced in the light over the scars on his red face. Beneteau had guessed right. But he had guessed wrong, too. It was a hundred yards across flat, open terrain to where they were laying out their bedrolls in a circle around the fire.

Beneteau wanted to crawl into the camp and pluck the cross right off the neck of the mean one while he slept. So confident was he, he didn't bring the Henry for protection. White men slept soundly in the fresh air when their confidence was reinforced by the strength of their numbers. They kept a single guard awake, but if a guard heard nothing moving in the darkness, he might not be alert. A snake could slither right through their camp and if it didn't rattle its buzz tail, no one would be wiser. But these posse men had chosen a spot surrounded by space. There was no way to sneak up on them. They had clear shooting at him for a hundred yards. From above their camp, he had misjudged the terrain. He wasn't even sure he could make it forward to the edge of blackness that formed where the glow of the fire faded. Buster padded softly to his back, crawled on it and came forward to nuzzle the nape of his neck. He reached around and pulled the coon to his side, gave it a gentle squeeze.

The camp grew still when the men turned in for the night. The guard fed the fire and leaned back against his saddle with a rifle across his midsection. Beneteau waited until the guard's head tilted his hat brim over his eyes, then he crept like a cougar toward his prey. Buster followed, but lost his playfulness. The coon mimicked the man friend. Where light from the flames began to lap at the blackness, Beneteau rose on his arms to confirm where his quarry was. He was convinced he could not make it into and out of the camp without being discovered. And he didn't even have a gun. It was a foolish waste of time. Beneteau could see a small canvas bag lying at the foot of the bearded man's bedroll. It might be for his personal belongings. He wanted the cross back. One try at least. He took the black play stone from his pocket and let Buster sniff it. He chucked it toward the sleeping man. Beneteau could not hear it hit the ground, but the guard's head came up and he looked around. Beneteau pushed his own face into the earth. The guard saw nothing within the circle of firelight and relaxed. Beneteau whispered encouragement to Buster who waddled after the stone. The coon's form was barely distinguishable from the earth to Beneteau as he watched the animal's progress. Buster's shape grew more distinct as it neared the campsite. Beneteau saw the coon wander near the sleeping man. The animal found the stone and started back. It stopped, sniffed, then ambled toward the bag. The coon seemed drawn by some other scent. He saw the little animal paw the bag and failing to get it open, tug at it. The guard's head lifted to look around, but saw nothing again. The coon dragged the bag back toward his man friend.

Beneteau reached forward to pull in the sack. Buster got a tasty meat treat from his other hand. Beneteau felt a hairy object in the bag, pulled it out and a patch of dried skin brushed against his face in the darkness. He knew it was a scalp lock. *That bastard*, he thought. The bag did not have anything in it heavy enough to be a gun. His fingers touched a leather thong and he tugged. He could tell by the object's lightness it was wood or bone and in the dark he felt its shape with his free hand.

Beneteau slipped the cross back over his neck, and he and the coon moved silently away into the deep shadows. They retraced their path to where Bronc stood tied and waiting.

Beneteau stifled a blood–curdling war cry that formed in his lungs. Having the cross back overshadowed not getting his Colt, too. The gun just backed up the luck he got from the cross. Buster caught the spirit of the moment and wiggled his way around the man's waist to his shirt front. The coon's black, moist nose pressed against the man's face in the darkness. Bronc shied almost unseating them. "Whoa," Beneteau said softly, steadying the horse. Buster trilled at the darkness. Beneteau got the horse quieted and jerked the Henry from its scabbard, cocking it noisily. The trail ahead seemed alive with activity. Beneteau could hear a grating noise. It seemed a dozen men were crawling ahead of them. The horse strained at the taut reins, its haunches quivering. Beneteau stared into the dark. Buster jumped behind him. Beneteau dismounted and pulled the horse's nose into the small of his back. He crouched and angled slowly toward the sound. He saw the movement and raised the rifle to his shoulder. A hefty chunk of willow slithered across the path in front of them, the branch pulled by a fat beaver. Beneteau uncocked the rifle and smiled. The busy animal ignored the three intruders and worked to tug the tree limb to its destination. The man remounted the horse. They needed to put as much distance as possible between themselves and the posse just in case they did figure out he and the raccoon had raided their camp. When they rode into open country, Beneteau let the piebald have its head, and the animal glided into a trot.

Beneteau thought of seeing Maria again. She was some pretty half breed woman. He had seen her naked once when he returned to the Turtles past Willow Creek with his saddle draped by freshly killed ducks. He hadn't snuck up on her. He just happened to be riding by and saw her step from a pool of water where she was bathing. She was seventeen then. She hadn't heard him, so he pulled up his horse and watched. She was humming, and her light, brown legs glistened in the sun and flowed upward to an exquisite appendage whose curves narrowed back at her waist and boughed back out again at her back like an hourglass. The lines faded where wet locks of black hair matted against her back. She flushed when she turned and saw him after she slipped into buckskin trousers. Too late, she clutched her tunic to her breasts. He had seen a lot of her and was not embarrassed by his forwardness.

"You pig!" she shouted at him.

Beneteau grinned and moved on slowly along the trail past her. She was like a beautiful berry begging to be plucked by gentle hands. Someday, she was going to get a lot of his attention.

Not long after the encounter, Maria flashed by on her pony. She quirted the animal to keep it at a full run, and she kept her dark eyes pinned on the ground in front of her. Even in her anger, Beneteau found himself admiring the view that tore past him. She stood in the stirrups, her torso bent over the pony's neck. If he had been a beaver, he would have smacked the water with his tail, so dangerously exciting did she appear. He thought he saw her look back his way when she disappeared on a bend.

Beneteau figured she must be nineteen now. *Men must be asking for her hand.* Maybe by the time he got back home, maybe she would be... He couldn't even form the thought in his mind that she might be taken by someone else.

A last quarter moon, the rising sun outlining its full shape from behind, stared back at him from a clear sky. Beneteau pulled up at the brow of a hill, dismounted and dug for grain in his saddlebag. Buster chattered beneath his legs as the coon pawed for the kernels that fell from Bronc's mouth. Beneteau got his pipe and sat down to smoke while he waited for the sun's deep orange shape to appear. The horizon was pink, then gold and it began to spread through the blackness where larger stars still sparkled brilliantly. Its beauty brought him a feeling he had watching Maria step out of Willow Creek. But now he looked for game. Hunger won his attention.

As daylight spread, Beneteau saw the light brown shapes of a band of pronghorns lying on a knoll a quarter mile away. He and Buster remounted and drifted back down the slope they were on to a gully downwind of the game animals. Beneteau tied the horse to a patch of sage, took the Henry and wrapped the eagle feather to the tip of its barrel. He commanded the coon to stay and set off afoot toward the animals, well out of range of the rifle. When he got to a spot in line with the antelope's view to the rising sun behind him, he crept up the bank of the gully and raised the feather–tipped rifle. The wind rustled the white and black feather. Beneteau lowered the gun and waited before raising it again to let the feather wiggle.

Beneteau brought the weapon down and pulled the hammer and waited. When he pushed himself into view, the curious antelope bolted from where they had wandered and stood to gaze transfixed on the fluttering feather. Beneteau singled out the closest pronghorn, fit him in the rifle's sights and sighted the gun ahead of the fleeing animal's form. He squeezed the trigger, heard the report and felt the impact slam into his shoulder. The young buck's white butt raised off the ground pushing its head and shoulders onto its forelegs. He ran to the downed animal, cut its throat and gutted it quickly before tossing it over his shoulders and carrying it back to the horse. He cut a strip of the tough flank meat and tossed it to Buster, then sliced another piece for himself which he chewed while he tied the carcass behind the saddle. He and Buster were mounted and went on their way to find a hiding place for their day camp. "We won't starve, pardner," he told the coon, who clung to his back with one hand while bouncing along atop the dead animal. Buster picked at the pronghorn's fur but couldn't get at any more fresh meat. Beneteau imagined the smell of antelope steak sizzling on a fire.

The raccoon trilled and tugged at the man's buckskin shirt as they passed a grove of buffalo berry bushes. The Henry was in Beneteau's hands as if thrust forward out of its scabbard by an unseen spirit hand. The gun's long, dark barrel swept the bush like an eagle's eye searching for prey.

Beneteau glinted over the sights, his eyes hardening on a lump that wasn't moving but appeared out of place.

Beneteau's thumb had drawn back the rifle's hammer, and he was ready to squeeze off a shot when the opening to the bush filled with a face. "Come out," Beneteau said.

Two hands parted the thatch surrounding the face. The hands were old and unsteady. As the being's head emerged, Beneteau saw locks of stringy, grey hair fall away to the being's shoulders. The weathered face of an old man emerged over a raggedy–clad frail body. He was Indian and leaned on a forked cottonwood limb as he continued to reveal his form.

"Don't gun me down in cold blood," the old Indian said in perfect English. "I'm not going to attack you. If I walloped you with this staff, you might be decent enough to lower that piece you've got trained on me."

Beneteau fumbled to park the rifle back in its scabbard. The old man was scrawny, but his dark eyes were clear and they darted from the horse, to the man, and to the raccoon while he gauged their demeanor.

"What are you doing out here, old one?" Beneteau said.

"Funny thing, young man, just before your arrival, I had been asking myself the same."

"Are you a Mandan?" Beneteau said, noticing that two small wooden canoes wobbled from wire circles that had pierced his ear lobes. The Mandans told the creation story about the Great Canoe bringing them to this land after a flood.

"Are you a white man?"

"I am Métis from the Turtle Mountains," Beneteau replied.

"I am a shaman," the old man said. "Until I had been taught to read by a white woman, I was being schooled to be a Medicine Man in my tribe, but now I know I am a *shaman*. The white woman called me that."

The old man looked harmless enough to Beneteau, who was off the horse and leading it to the bushes where he tied it. Buster, too, had crawled down and was circling the old man warily.

"Skeedaddle, you vermin," the old man shouted when Buster fondled the tattered hem of his cloth robe.

"You speak good English," Beneteau said.

"I should; I am a learned shaman."

"You haven't said what you are doing?"

"I am too hungry to talk," the old man replied, eying the antelope carcass.

"Is this your camp?"

"No, my home is in that hill." He pointed to where sandstone rocks had eroded until their ends had broken and slid into heaps in a gully. He hobbled off toward the hill with Buster chattering along at his heels. Beneteau followed.

When Buster sank his teeth into the trailing robe, the old man turned and swung at the raccoon with his staff. The old man's moves were defensive, the animal's more playful than aggressive. Beneteau followed until they came to the entrance to the shaman's home. The old man picked his way up a path and disappeared behind a wide, flat hunk of the sandstone. Buster waited for the man friend to stake the horse and lug the antelope up the hill.

When they walked around the stone, they found the old man with kindling he gathered for a fire and he was hitting a flint rock against a strip of metal. A tuft of rabbit hair sent up a small trail of smoke, which the old man fanned with his bony hand. Flames flickered and he fed them with small twigs and tufts of dried grass.

Without more talk, Beneteau busied himself separating the hindquarters of meat from the rest of the antelope. He hacked through the backbone and came up with a rack of ribs and a foot-long section of the animal's loin. The old man's fire glowed as Beneteau speared the meat on the willow spit.

"Have you any coffee?" the shaman said. "Hog crap," he muttered when Beneteau shook his head. Then, he disappeared in his cave and reappeared with a fruit tin which he hung over the blaze. Beneteau saw coffee grounds floating atop water the old man had poured into the tin.

Beneteau got the pipe from his saddlebag, tapped it full of tobacco and offered it to the shaman.

"The white men taught me not to smoke before eating." But he took the long-stemmed, red-stone pipe and lifted it to the Four Directions and the Above and Mother Earth and drew on it before passing it back to Beneteau. "I was brought up to offer my prayers to the Creator before doing anything on this earth."

The aroma from the antelope spread in the shelter, then escaped to the blue sky above them. Beneteau offered his knife to his host, and the old man separated two ribs from the rest and cut to the spine. He wrestled with the meat until Beneteau took the knife and whacked it loose.

Each man gnawed at the rich meat without a word. The old man offered Beneteau a tin cup. He dipped his in the coffee can and Beneteau did likewise. The fire warmed the squatting space until a pleasant atmosphere existed among the two crouching humans and raccoon.

Beneteau filled the pipe again and this time drew on it for the pure joy of the smoke coming into his body.

"Your wrists tell me you have had an adventure you might not want to talk about," the old man said, nibbling a bone as he eyed the wounds. "Maybe you are a man with a price on his head?"

"You are prying like an old woman," Beneteau replied. "You have eaten my meat, and I would expect better from you."

"It is only because the wrists are so noticeable."

"Your skinny hide is noticeable, too, but I did not ask you how it got that way."

"Forgive me. Even an old man can forget his upbringing. I was also schooled by Jesuits after the white widow woman taught me to read. The priests were always prying, looking for sins to whip out of one. I speak better English now than my own language. The Mandan tongue was a sin to speak."

"The Métis were forbidden to speak Michif, too. But we spoke it all the time when the priests weren't around," Beneteau said. His wrists ached anew from the attention.

The shaman sensed his discomfort. "I have something that may make them feel better," he said, before disappearing inside his cave. He returned with a buffalo horn from which he dipped a goo on the fingers of his right hand. "This will sooth those wrists," the old man said, whistling through the spaces in his teeth.

Beneteau held out his arms while the shaman dabbed the ointment on his wrists. He winced, but the mixture soothed as it soaked in his skin.

"What is the magic potion?" he said to the old man, who sat back and hummed an Indian melody.

"Skunk fat," the shaman said.

"You old bastard," Beneteau said, starting to wipe the goo from his wrists.

"No, no," said the old man. "That is a healer that few know about. It is better than bear grease."

Beneteau's wrists felt caressed as the goo soaked his skin.

"What is your name?" The question posed by the shaman hung in the air, unanswered. "Oh, I suppose you would like to know who wants to know. My name is Bunny."

"Used to be Rabbit, Horace Rabbit, before that woman got me and changed it."

Beneteau stretched forward to shake the bony hand extended by the shaman. "The Sioux call me Hinanska, White Owl. but to my own people I am known as *D'or Métis, the Golden Métis*."

"Horace," said the shaman, "my full Christian name is Horace Throckmorton Bunny."

"My Christian name is Phillipe Antoine Beneteau," Beneteau said, embarrassed by the shaman's formality. "I thought you said you are Mandan."

"I am a Mandan, a holy Mandan, but once I learned I was a shaman I have never used my real Indian name. My full name is Horace Throckmorton Bunny the third."

"Why are you so proud of being a shaman?" Beneteau said, trying to end the old man extending his name further.

"I have found that white people are intrigued by Indian life, but have no stomach to live it. Once I learned to read and write, I took to writing down for any who would read the stories of my tribe and how I could doctor the people with medicines the Creator provided."

"And the white people were *interested*?"

"Yes. Take you, for instance, what do you know about the Mandan Indians? I'll wager, scarcely a thing. Yet, the Mandans lived here before the French came and, even before the Athabascans, from which the Chippewas descend."

"Says who?" Beneteau said, annoyed by the old man's tone.

"If you spent more time reading and less time watching, you would appreciate what I am talking about."

"I am not impressed by old men who live like a badger in a cave," Beneteau said.

"You ride alone. Well, practically alone except for the animal."

"Buster," Beneteau said.

"Buster then. You, ride alone and apparently have no appreciation for the freedom of thought that comes from solitude."

"I travel faster alone," said Beneteau.

"So do I," said the old man, "but I travel with my mind by thoughts that I take in and give back to writing paper."

"It is great that you live your life in a cave and put your thoughts on paper. I live my life by my wits and back my thoughts with action."

"So I have noticed," the old man said. Beneteau's wrists glistened an eery green in the light from the fire.

Beneteau felt like he was in a classroom and had come unprepared for the day's lesson. This scrawny old man made him feel inferior. He didn't even like animals. Could you imagine, an Indian Medicine Man who didn't even like the four-leggeds? The whites had twisted his mind.

"Old one, if you are so learned, why do you waste your time in a cave?"

"You have never heard of Saint John the Baptist, I presume," the old man replied. "You have read the Bible? Probably not. You were probably spoon fed everything you learned by nuns."

"I wasn't spoon fed anything," Beneteau said.

"Saint John was a holy man in the time of Jesus Christ. He lived in a cave in the desert and preached the coming of the Lord."

"I have patterned my life after his, but whites won't call an Indian a prophet."

"Have you ever had a woman?" Beneteau asked.

"No. Saint John would never degrade his life by taking up with a woman. He was a celibate."

"Celibate," Beneteau said. "That's a new one for me."

"They did not cavort with women," the old man said.

"*Cavort with women*," Beneteau said. "You mean they lived their lives without crawling in bed with a woman? Are you a man–lover?"

"No, no. A celibate devotes his life to a higher calling, serving the Creator."

"Like a priest, then."

"No, more holy than a priest, who lives with the comforts of man and may even sleep with a woman."

"You make yourself sound special," Beneteau said.

"I am special. It was you who brought me meat to eat and now I give you the bread of life."

Beneteau remained puzzled by the old man. He must have lost his mind in his solitude.

"The Creator brought you to serve me."

"Not for long. I'll be leaving shortly."

"You don't understand, Mr. Beneteau. I am a shaman and you have come to serve my needs."

"Buster, he doesn't understand," Beneteau said, turning to the raccoon. "Sorry, I already work for the raccoon."

"Hogwash! You couldn't possibly be indebted to an animal above a shaman."

"Show him who is the boss, Buster," Beneteau said.

The raccoon ran a circle around the two sitting men. The shaman's eyes widened. Buster slowed and rose on his hind legs to pirouette, then the animal stooped and threw two handfuls of sand on his head. He charged the old man, hitting against his shoulder and nearly toppling him over on his side. The animal careened back to the ground and spun around to do the same trick to Beneteau, who sat roaring with laughter.

"Enough, enough," said the old man. "You are free of my powers."

"*Ayaw*!" Beneteau commanded, and Buster calmed down but without restraint on his chattering. "I would have thought a man of your learning would have had something more important to tell me than what I've heard," Beneteau said.

"You are slow to learn, my son. I give you one of the most important lessons in your life; yet, you miss the point."

"You haven't given me anything. I have given you meat and taught you that even a raccoon isn't afraid of you."

"I will agree with you that you have a mind of your own, that you are different from your run–of–the–mill half breed. You look white. You could even pass for a Mandan."

"No, I couldn't pass for a Mandan. My hair is fair, but my eyes are not blue enough."

“Heh, and you exhibit a flare for the search for knowledge, or you wouldn’t even comprehend my comparison between you and my people.”

“So, what is the big point that I missed from this chance meeting with an old man living in a cave?”

“You have missed the point that you should never trust anyone, especially a shaman,” the old man said, revealing a double–barreled Derringer he had trained on Beneteau’s midsection from beneath his robe.

“I need a horse to get out of this god–forsaken country and back to civilization in St. Louis.”

“You old muskrat!” Beneteau said, his green wrists rising with his hands above his head.

Chapter 4

The black holes of the nickel–plated gun glared at Beneteau, who raised his hands before opening his mouth. “You have lived among the white man longer than I thought,” he said.

“Yes,” said Horace. “The whites have taught me well. If a white man wants something, he simply takes it. If anyone stands in his way, he kills him.”

“Do you intend to kill me?”

“There isn’t any point in discussing your predicament. One might ask is there any reason you should be allowed to live? I can’t think of one.”

“I thought you were a shaman, not a robber or killer.”

“You thought, you thought,” the old man said. “Exactly the point. You didn’t think. You see, Mr. Beneteau, when I told you that I had become a shaman and that you had come to serve me—even then, you couldn’t understand.”

“I understood. You seemed kind of loco. Now, you have a gun and what you said makes a lot more sense.”

"Would that you were red man enough to die like a warrior. When I have the upper hand, you take on the traits of a white man and start to cower. You only understand power—the power of the gun."

Beneteau's cheek muscles twitched. Not only had the old man got the drop on him, but now he even hoped he was ready to beg for his life. Why would this old person want to kill him? For his horse? It could have been the other way. He could have shot the old buzzard in the brush, even justified it in his mind. How could he have known that it was just an old man hiding in some bushes? If he didn't tell anyone, no one would ever know except himself that he had killed an old one.

The shaman tilted the Derringer skyward at an angle above Beneteau's face.

"Let's see if this thing works," he said, pressing his finger against the forward trigger. The gun recoiled in his hand as the bullet sped into the air in front of Beneteau's face, blasted by powder.

Beneteau winced, then watched the gun drop back level with his chest at a spot where his heart thumped. The shaman drew back the hammer of the second barrel as the gun returned to its position, and Beneteau saw the old man's bony finger press the rear trigger. He waited for the slug's impact. Thoughts about his life thundered like a herd of buffalo through his mind. **AT THE AGE OF 26, PHILLIPE ANTOINE BENETEAU DIED ON THE PRAIRIE GRASSLANDS OF DAKOTA WITH LESS DIGNITY THAN AN INDIAN WOULD GIVE A BADGER.** The click of the hammer falling echoed in his mind. But it was just the click. The hammer fell on an empty cylinder.

"Now, let us see if you have learned anything, or must be taught another lesson," the shaman said.

Beneteau was ready to pounce on the old man's frail frame and murder him, but the old one could have killed him.

"Okay, Mr. Bunny. I have been sent by the Creator to serve you. What do you want me to do?"

"First, let me get rid of this thing," the old man said. He dropped the hammer of another Derringer he was holding concealed under his robe in his other hand, then stuffed both into little holsters on a leather belt that had been hidden by his tattered outer garment.

"I thought you might need another lesson."

Beneteau shook his head.

"You do not have much time to spend with me. That is why you must listen closely to what I have to tell you. White Owl, it is very important for you to always remember that when Mother Earth gives you something, it comes from the Creator. Not just for you, but for other creatures. The gifts given so freely, must be shared in a like manner. You were not made my master by bringing the antelope here for us to eat. And I was not made your master because I am a shaman with guns. Two–leggeds are all brothers and sisters. The whites are good, just as reds, yellows and blacks. Only when one human being tries to dominate another do we human's make trouble for the rest. No one should look down on the Creator's work. There can be peace and harmony in this world."

Beneteau watched the old man shake flakes of tobacco into a piece of scrap paper he then fashioned into an ungainly cigarette. He leaned to the fire and the paper flared, then began to smoke, causing the old man's eye to water where the smoke curled past it.

"I am still hungry," he said, his head shaking his grey hair from side to side along his bony shoulders.

"What is it you want me to do?" Beneteau asked. "Take my horse for your ride back to St. Louis if you want it."

"No, I don't want your horse. I may move from here in the future, but this is my home. I do not really want to go to St. Louis. I am a shaman and *have to do what I have to do.*"

Buster watched the two men. He chattered when Beneteau handed the old man a piece of antelope he had tugged from the willow spit over the fire. The coon made for the meat.

"Get away, you dratted scavenger." the old man said, clutching his meat and pulling back from Buster.

The coon jumped on his lap and stretched for a treat, the animal somehow sensing the old one was not as mean as he tried to act.

"Okay, here's a bite. But no more and please, Mr. Beneteau, try to get your friend to act with some semblance of decency."

"Noo!" Beneteau commanded. Buster waddled to a spot near Beneteau where the animal sat munching his mooched treat.

The wind was building. When Beneteau got up and peered around the stone wall shielding the entrance to the shaman's cave, he could see lightning illuminating dark clouds rolling in from the horizon. He returned to the fire.

"A storm is coming."

"In life, Mr. Beneteau, a storm is always coming. The Creator is testing our mettle."

The cold wind rushing across the plains swirled around the stone barrier scattering sparks. The old man entered the cave and came back with a sheet of bent tin, discarded probably by a passing settler. He laid it like a lean-to over the top of the fire.

"I'll gather fuel and tend to my horse," Beneteau said, getting up to leave.

The shaman ignored him and piled stones on the edge of the tin where it touched the ground. Beneteau returned with an armload of buffalo chips and chunks of dried wood he found scattered in the brush. On his second trip he toted his saddle and saddlebags. The old one motioned for him to stow the gear in the cave. Then the two men sat back down and listened to the howl of the wind. Beneteau sought permission to enter the shaman's cave.

"Go ahead, Mr. Beneteau. My home is your home," the old man said, but he did not move out of the open area. Beneteau felt the warmth inside radiating off the tin the shaman had put in place. He threw the saddle blanket down and put his saddle on it, then unrolled his bed and laid with his head on the saddle. He noticed the old man looked skyward and his lips moved. Thunder boomed in back of a flash of lightning. The storm rolled in fast. A few large drops of rain splattered on the ground in little puffs of dust, then the sky darkened except for scattered lightning and explosions of thunder. Still, the old man sat outside and prayed. Beneteau was about to call him in, when lightning streaked from the sky into the tin over the fire, then ricocheted into the ground. The shaman's hair flew straight out from his head across his shoulders and his body quivered before he toppled face down in the wet dirt.

Beneteau jumped up and crawled on hands and knees to the old man. He tugged and dragged him into the cave. The old one's body felt clammy and still. He laid the frail frame on his bedroll, his head propped up by the saddle. Beneteau looked around the dim interior and saw a tin bucket on a slab of sandstone near the cave entrance. He crawled to it. It was half full of water. He brought it back to the still form of the old man and dumped the water on his grey head. Beneteau would have bet the shaman was dead, but he would have bet more that he saw his face twitch when the water splashed over him. The storm outside had settled down to a steady hard rain. Cool air mixed with heat from the sputtering embers of the fire. Beneteau pulled his oil slicker over the old man. He picked up a cottonwood pole from a pile the old one had stashed in the cave and pushed it through the cave entrance into the fire. The flames bit into the dry wood and flared. Beneteau crawled back to the old man and touched his forehead, which was still cold and ashen in color. He thought of praying. The old man had seemed to want to tell him something, yet had not had a chance to say much. Buster waddled over by his man friend, who stroked the coon's fur. Beneteau gave him a hug.

"Looks like it is just you and me again, pardner." The coon trilled, but began to sniff the old man's body. He nudged it with haziness, then poked at it with his black leathery paws. The little animal ambled along the length of the old one's prostrate frame, chattering as he explored.

"I think he's a goner," Beneteau said to the coon. Buster sniffed the old man's face, his wet nose pressed against the peaked nose of the old man. The coon pushed his nose into one of the old man's nostrils.

"Confound that miserable beast!" the old man said in a hoarse voice. "Scat! Get away from me!"

Buster retreated to his man friend.

"You are alive," said Beneteau.

"Of course I am alive. Why shouldn't I be?"

"You don't remember anything?"

"Certainly. I was sleeping. Then your cursed animal woke me."

"No, no, Mr. Bunny. You were sitting by the fire in the storm, praying, I think. A bolt of lightning almost hit you. I thought you were dead."

"No wonder my body aches. I thought it was the lumbago. *Ha*, the Creator has given us more to ponder. It is He, you know, who brings the thunder beings. I was praying that you would become enlightened, Mr. Beneteau."

“Can I get you anything?”

“I still have an empty spot in my stomach. I’d have another slice of antelope steak.”

Beneteau slipped from the cave and brought back the meat that had been slow cooking under the tin. They each ate another slab and Buster got chunks of the tasty meat handed to him on the point of Beneteau’s knife. It had grown dark outside and the hard rain had turned into a drizzle as Beneteau pushed the wood further into the fire. The old one sat up to eat his meat, then sank prone again and closed his eyes. Beneteau and Buster curled up on a piece of canvas the old man used for a bed. Beneteau pulled half of the stiff cloth over them and they were all still in the shaman’s cavern.

When he awoke, Beneteau noticed that both the old man and Buster were gone. Daylight streamed through the cave entrance. The fire was going, minus the tin roof and the tin can was steaming where it was hooked over the spit. Beneteau could smell coffee, but the fireplace was deserted. He rolled to his hands and knees and crawled through the opening. When he look around the rock slab, Beneteau saw the old one, his robe flowing, trudging slowly back to the cave. Buster was at his side. The old man was carrying willow rods on his back. Beneteau trod down the path to meet them.

“Let me give you a hand,” he said as the two approached.

“If you would give me a hand, go to the thicket in which you first found me and bring the other bundle of willows.”

“What is your plan, Mr. Bunny?”

The old man paused, breathed deep and looked into Beneteau’s hazel eyes.

“I am trying to get you to listen. I have made a statement of how you could be of assistance. But you think you are a shaman and ask my intentions.”

"Okay, okay. I'll get the damned willows."

Buster ignored Beneteau in favor of trailing along with the old man and his fascinating robe. The coon let the cloth brush against him, but did not hang on it.

By the time Beneteau returned with the rest of the willows, the shaman had the framework of a sweat lodge built.

"You know what this is I presume, Mr. White Owl Beneteau?"

"Yes." Beneteau replied, solemnly.

He had not been in a sweat lodge for years. The priests had told the Métis it was a waste of time and energy. Some of the old men still slipped away from the Métis settlement to sweats hidden in the trees. But Beneteau himself had not been in one since he was ten.

"Perhaps," the shaman told him, "you can go on the other side of this hill and gather gifts from Stone Boy."

"Stone Boy?"

"Yes, there is a pile of round granite stones left by Stone Boy in an old fire pit on the slope away from where we are. Make a container and bring them back to me." Beneteau took the piece of canvas he had slept on in the cave, flung it over his shoulder and went in search of the stones. He found them, placed fifteen of the stones in the sack he made and returned to the old man, who now stood with his tin bucket dangling in his hand at the end of a bony arm.

"Just place the stones there by the fire," the old one said. "Then, take this bucket to the willow thicket and at the rear of the bushes you will find a pool of water I have dug from a small spring. Fill this bucket and return."

Buster had become so fascinated by the old man, he stayed back while Beneteau went for the water. The animal hung on the ribs of the lodge that was being built and drew a curse from the shaman whenever the frail structure sagged dangerously under the animal's weight. Yet, the old one never touched the critter and slowly the willow lodge was tied together by coarse lengths of grass the old man carried in a little sheath that hung on his shoulder. When Beneteau returned this time, the rocks were heating in the fire and the old man had dug a pit in the center of the sweat lodge. Under his direction, Beneteau aided in covering the lodge with their bedding, his slicker, saddle blanket—every available sheet of material. Then, the old one set about to fill in any openings with the branches that had been removed from the willow stems. Beneteau helped. When he paused and tried to dip himself a cup of coffee, the old one ordered him not to drink anything, nor eat.

"First, we must become pure of mind and spirit," the shaman said.

When the stones were hot, the old man laid out two thick poles side by side. He rolled four stones into the cradle the sticks formed and bid Beneteau raise one end carefully, while he took the other two and entered the lodge. He set his side down at the edge of the pit and told Beneteau to raise his ends slowly. The stones rolled into the pit and they repeated the act with three more stones.

"Undress now and enter," the shaman said.

Beneteau did as directed, then sat and watched the old man's form darken the entrance. He brought the bucket and set it beside him. Buster could not be kept outside and tumbled in after the old man, then took up a position between the two humans.

The old one's bony arm pulled the lodge flap closed and he began a low chant. Beneteau crossed himself. He worried the steam would eat away the skunk grease protecting his wrists and sear them with pain.

At the first splash of water, steam hissed in the darkness. With each succeeding cupful of water, the heat rose inside the lodge. Beneteau started once to speak, but the hot air rushed into his mouth and he almost choked on it. The old man had stopped chanting. They could hear Buster clawing at the under edge of the lodge. Still, the old one heaped more water and hotter steam filled the lodge. Sweat gushed from Beneteau's forehead, his back and chest, down his thighs until the ground he sat on seemed soaked.

When the old man finally threw open the flap to let cool air flow in, Buster shot through the opening.

"You are one of the Creator's fine blessings, varmint, but you are not his highest. The highest are two–leggeds and we have a long way to travel on this warm road before we can escape as you have done."

He pulled the flap shut and Beneteau could feel the heat build again. His wrists burned, but the grease had penetrated and his skin was soft, though tender.

The shaman went through the ceremony four times, before he released Beneteau to visit the water pool where he could dip water over his scorched body. The old man said he would air dry himself and let the wind carry off the excess heat in his body.

Beneteau couldn't explain to himself why he felt so good. He just did. He felt like running and slipped into a jog. He carried his pants in one hand, the water gourd in the other. It was so exhilarating that by the time he reached the brush where the water pool was hidden, he simply dropped his pants and the gourd at the edge of thicket and broke into a full-fledge romp with his arms hanging loosely at his sides. Cool air brushed against his muscular body, stimulating him to even greater speed. His bare feet padded on the ground and he followed a game path that led down a wash and curved between two round hills before it cut to an eroded bank he flew down.

Before he could complete his plan to circle the hills, regain the game path and return to the thicket to bathe, Beneteau was confronted by two buffalo bulls locked head to head and grunting at each other. The younger of the two bulls bolted at the first sight of the naked human. The old one, mucous trailing from its flaring nostrils, bent its neck to watch the man with its dark eyes.

Beneteau, bucking to a dead standstill, saw the old bull's tail arched like a figure seven and he was already turning to strike out in the opposite direction when what he knew would happen did.

The buffalo, pawed up a cloud of dust and lit out after the man, whose white buttocks seemed to beckon to the giant beast.

Up to now, Beneteau had just been loping for fun and enjoying himself. The bull spooked him, to full stride. Beneteau expected to be lifted off the ground by the big bull's black horns. He dodged left, then right at the first touch by the great beast. The bull moaned, his hoof beats pounding louder.

Beneteau felt the animal's breath on his posterior and he strove to outdistance his pursuer. The bull stretched to hook him but its hindquarters buckled. The young bull had returned to attack his foe in the rear, too.

By the time Beneteau reached the thicket and flung himself into it to retrieve his pants and the gourd, the two bulls were back at each other in a cloud of dust. Beneteau doused himself with water from the shaman's pool, pulled on his trousers and emerged under the gaze of the old man and the raccoon who had watched all from a perch near the old man's cave.

Buster chattered at his man friend.

"Mr. Beneteau, I see the Creator has given you another lesson in life. One should never take anything for granted. You flee beautifully."

"I suppose you wouldn't have run?"

"An interesting thought. Had you not the ability to run, you would have had neither the misfortune of loping into those two kings of the prairie, nor the speed with which to retreat. Mr. Beneteau, you have much to learn and so little time. I thank the Creator for helping out."

"If you are so wise, why do you have to carry guns?" Beneteau said.

"Guns are not my stock in trade, sir. I am a man of learning. I have never shot anything in my life."

"Maybe not, but you eat antelope like a mountain lion. Somebody has to put them down. If everybody was like you, we'd all be eating grass."

"There will come a day," the old said, "there will come a day..." His voiced trailed off and his eyes raised to the brow of a hill a quarter mile distant from the cave dwelling. "It appears we will be having company. I hope you have time to finish clothing yourself, Mr. Beneteau."

Seven braves sat astride horses staring at them from the brow of the hill. Beneteau slipped into his tunic and pulled on his moccasins. He reached for the Henry.

"There, there, White Owl, let me handle this," said the shaman, grabbing his walking pole and strolling toward the Indians. His tattered robe trailed behind him, and Buster waddled along after it. Beneteau slipped behind the cave's entrance to a position that allowed him to use it for a stationary rifle rest. He watched the old man near the midway point to the warriors.

The lance–carrying leader of the group, lowered the feather-tipped point and dug his heels into the ribs of his pony. The seven Indians split four left, three right and charged on an arch toward the old man and the raccoon.

Beneteau raised the Henry to its rest, then sighted along the barrel toward the lance bearer.

The old man stopped and waited. One of the warriors uncoiled a rawhide lariat and as they swept past the shaman he dropped a noose over his torso. The old one was jerked from his feet and a puff of dust ascended where his body banged into the ground. Buster watched the warriors race away.

The Henry barked in Beneteau's hands and the warrior who was dragging the old man recoiled and dropped from his horse. The motionless bodies of the old one and the fallen Indian were lumps behind the other warriors who continued to race across the prairie. Beneteau fired another round at the lance–bearer and he, too, fell from his horse's back, but he rolled to his feet and was quickly picked up by two of the others. The Indians formed a single line and struck out away from the small battle-field without turning back.

By the time Beneteau got to the shaman, his body was moving. Between moans, he looked up when Beneteau approached.

"Damned Oglala!" he said. "You never can trust a cutthroat Sioux. I thought I could use my power on them, but they are too hardheaded."

Beneteau checked out the fallen warrior, then returned to the old one. The shaman sat up and brushed dirt from his face. Buster joined them.

"Is he dead?" the old one asked of the fallen Indian.

"Yes," said Beneteau, nudging the body with the Henry's barrel.

"Then we must build a scaffold for his burial. The Sioux would like that. Perhaps, they will even learn a lesson from this. I think they knew I was a Mandan. Please, Mr. Beneteau, take care of your miserable beast."

Buster was sniffing the old man around the ears and touching him on the frail chest where light wounds oozed blood.

Beneteau helped the old man to his feet and supported him as they returned to the cave. His eyes swept the land around them, but the small war party was gone.

"The Creator is always testing us," the shaman said. "I learned that from the Jesuits."

"I sure am glad they made you so wise, Mr. Bunny," Beneteau said. Buster trotted between their legs and grabbed at the old man's robe.

Chapter 5

Beneteau thought it a mite crazy that he and the old man should waste their time building a scaffold for the dead warrior. But Horace Throckmorton Bunny III was adamant. The shaman didn't want to leave his home, and he doubted the Sioux would return to claim their fallen comrade if Beneteau and his Henry were still visitors.

The two men grunted to get the wrapped body of the warrior up on the platform. The Sioux's only possessions were his bow, arrows, knife and the rawhide lariat he had used to rope the old man. They wrapped his body in a frayed piece of canvas that had been used to build the sweat lodge. His belongings were laid ceremonially around his head, positioned with his face to the east.

"I think that both the Creator and the Sioux will be pleased by this act," the old man said.

"You may be right," Beneteau said, squinting his eyes toward movement appearing at the skyline. "It looks like they've sent some warriors to praise our work."

The old man looked where Beneteau was focused. Dust flared behind a war party of 20 Sioux, headed toward the two men at the base of the scaffold.

"We better hurry back to my place," the shaman said, hobbling off toward the cave with Buster bobbing along with him.

Beneteau grabbed up his Henry, but went to his horse which he caught and led at a trot to the cave.

"You're planning to run," the old man said when he saw Beneteau toss his saddle blanket on the piebald, then the saddle, which he cinched tight.

The Sioux shapes grew larger on the horizon above their loping ponies. The warriors' feathered lances danced vertically above their bobbing forms.

"No. We're planning to run," he said emphasizing the plural and swinging into the saddle. He stretched his foot down for Buster to climb up to the stirrup.

"In front," he told Buster, then he dropped his left arm and foot to the old man. "C'mon."

The shaman raised his arm to protest and Beneteau grabbed it as he spurred the horse. The old man dangled precariously, got his leg up high enough to meet Beneteau's foot with his own and swung in an arch behind the saddle's cantle. The big horse was at full stride before the approaching warriors reacted. Beneteau saw their lances dip forward with their charge. Their war cries were faint, but chilling.

"We can't outrun them," the old one said.

"We sure as hell can't talk our way out of this," Beneteau said over his shoulder.

"You didn't have to kill that warrior," the shaman shouted into the back of Beneteau's neck.

"I wish I was as smart as you," Beneteau said. "If you don't shut up and hang on, you may get a chance to make peace with those Sioux."

The raccoon had turned his back on the wind breaking around the horse's neck and gripped Beneteau's shirt front with his paws. His bushy tail waved from side to side, sometimes brushing his man friend's face and obstructing his vision.

The old man's long, grey hair and the ends of his ragged cloak flared back over the horse's rump. His bare, bony arms made it possible to rivet his hands to Beneteau's sides.

Beneteau was confident Bronc could outrun the Indian ponies without the old man. With him, the odds were weighted against escape. The old man was pretty scrawny, barely worth saving.

"White Owl, the Creator has given us another test. You are a lucky man to have met me."

"You bet," Beneteau said, hooking his right arm over Buster's tail and clenching it to his side.

"The white people are building a village over there," the old man said, pointing with his bony fingers past Beneteau's head to the west. "They call it Pleasant Valley."

Bronc ran with ease, putting distance between them and the Indians. Beneteau knew that if he had to fight, he could make a good stand against the poorly armed Sioux with the 14 shots he carried in the Henry. The Indians, seeing the futility of the chase by the direction their prey fled, pulled up on the brow of a distant hill and watched them fade on the horizon.

Darkness spread even as the threesome climbed to high ground and viewed the small town below. Beneteau saw lantern lights flickering in the scattered wooden buildings.

"It doesn't look too pleasant to me," Beneteau said.

"One can never be sure with whites," the old man said.

"I say we circle and make a camp on the north side," Beneteau said.

"I'm starving," the old man replied.

They skirted the little town until they came to a small creek. Stars eased out of the sky by the time Beneteau pulled the piebald up and unloaded.

Once the old man and Buster were on the ground, Beneteau got off and led the horse to a patch of buffalo berry bushes. He slipped the bit from his horse's mouth and tied him loosely to a branch. He took his saddlebags and rejoined Horace who was making a campfire.

"What do we have for grub?" the old man said when he approached.

Beneteau dropped the saddlebags, crouched beside them and withdrew a small parcel which he unwrapped.

"We're down to the last of my pemmican," he said, offering the meal to Horace.

The raccoon danced forward in the firelight and snatched a portion of the morsel the old man had taken between his thumb and forefinger.

"That's it. The animal goes, or I go," he said, cupping his other hand around the pemmican. Buster wobbled away to Beneteau and sat there nibbling his treat. Beneteau ignored the comment.

"Sure wish we had some of your coffee," he said.

"Ah, Mr. White Owl, you thought me a fool," the old man said, pushing back his robe to expose the rawhide pouch he had tied to the sash holding up his breechcloth.

"We have no pot for water," Beneteau said.

"Try this," the old man said, taking a pinch of the coffee and sticking it inside his lower lip like a chew of snuff.

Beneteau did and felt the pleasant taste spread through his taste buds and into his body. After a bit of staring into the fire, he got the stone pipe and tapped it full of tobacco. He lit the pipe with a small twig he inserted in the fire and offered it to the old man.

"Oh, mighty Creator, who has given us all things, thank you for this day and all you have taught us," the shaman said, raising the pipe to the sky. Chanting in Mandan, he pointed to each of the four directions, then down to Mother Earth before he sat down and drew smoke from its stem.

"The Sioux taught us this," he said. "They are a strong, beautiful people."

"If you are such good friends, why did they try to drag you off?"

"Ah, Mr. Beneteau, you jumped to a bad conclusion back there. Those Indians tried to get me out of that cave for a month. They said it was a Wakan place. A war party was ambushed there by Crows once, and the Sioux said the cave was the tomb of the dead warriors' spirits."

"They would have killed you."

"Only if the Creator allowed it. I was just having a hard time convincing those Sioux that I was holy enough to be there."

Beneteau shook his head and rubbed Buster's back.

"In the morning, I'll slip into town and see if I can get us some fresh supplies," he told the old man.

"You think it wouldn't be wise for me to go along?"

"Never know. I always feel uneasy even though they think I'm white."

"Do what you think is best, White Owl."

The two men turned in for the night, Buster snuggling up beside his man friend. The old man was still chanting lowly when Beneteau dozed off.

In the morning, a snipe darting above whistled them awake at dawn. Beneteau put on his boots and took his feather from the band of his flat–brimmed hat. He saddled Bronc and told the old man to keep an eye on Buster.

"I know you don't always get on real good with this guy," he said, nodding toward the raccoon who was busy washing himself with his front paws. "But he is my best friend. I hope you can understand that."

The old man scowled, but didn't retreat when Buster came toward him to pull on the end of his robe.

"I'll be back as quick as I can," Beneteau said, spurring the piebald into an easy canter in the direction of the small town they had passed in the night.

The town was further south of their camp than he thought, but soon the man and horse arrived on a hill from which he could see the forms of settlers moving. By the time he got to the outskirts, smoke was curling from chimneys and wagons were rumbling on the small settlement's dirt streets.

"Howdy," Beneteau nodded, as he passed a buckboard headed north on the rutted trail. The two men seated behind a team of big black work horses appeared to be farmers. Whatever they were hauling was hidden from sight by a weathered, grey tarpaulin. They nodded to him and Beneteau heard them exchange comments in German, a language he wasn't familiar with. The words were guttural and came out of their mouths harshly. They were thickset men and wore flat hats that had brims only over their foreheads.

Beneteau rode his horse onto the grass hump left in the middle where wagon wheels had cut into the prairie grass. The road stretched toward a weathered building whose two wide doors had been flung open. He could hear a metal hammer pinging off a steel anvil. Acrid smoke from a blacksmith's coals burned his nasal passages.

Beneteau rode to the building and dismounted. A huge man, biceps bared beneath cut–off shirtsleeves, was shaping a red hot horseshoe on the anvil. He wore a dirty rawhide apron and his head was bald and beaded with sweat.

"What can I do for you?" the smith said when Beneteau stood in the doorway.

"I was just passing through and looking for any work that might stake me to a little grub," Beneteau told him.

The smith looked at Beneteau's slim build and shook his head.

"Don't look to me like you know much about this kind of work. What can you do?"

"I can chop a fine pile of wood," he answered. Cottonwoods were stacked on the side of the smith's shop. A double-bladed ax was buried in a stump that was marred by bites from its blade.

"Yeh," the big man said. "You might be able to handle a job like that. I'll give you two bits for every cord of wood you cut and stack."

Beneteau tied into the logs and by noon had two eight-foot-long cords in place. The smith paid him and Beneteau got permission to leave his horse behind the shop while he walked uptown.

The shopkeeper looked him over carefully when he entered.

"New in town?" the man said.

"Just passing through," Beneteau told him. "I'd like to get a little flour and bacon. "'Bout fifty cents worth."

"Have a container?"

Beneteau unstrapped the rawhide bag he had over his shoulder. "Just put it in here. Be fine."

The shopkeeper tipped the bag over and banged its sides on a trash bucket on the floor. A cartridge wedged in the seam popped out and clanked in the bucket.

"Forty–four," said the shopkeeper. "You carry a forty–four?"

"Just put that flour and bacon right in here and everything will be just fine," Beneteau said. He knew white etiquette well enough to know the shopkeeper was just nosy.

Beneteau's boots echoed hollowly on the store's board floor when he left. The wooden door creaked as it swung closed behind him when he stepped out to the street. He was distracted by motion off to his left. Two men came out of the hotel and readied their horses. He recognized the man called Cal and the mean one who had taken his Colt. Beneteau slid between the walls of the store and another building and watched the two mount and ride north out of town.

He hurried down a side street toward the edge of the new village to the smith's shop.

"More wood to chop if you want," the smith said, when he walked in front of the gaping opening which gushed out smoke and heat from the forge.

"I'd like to stay on, but I have to be going," Beneteau said.

"Suit yourself."

Bronc was nibbling grass when Beneteau pulled him up on the halter rope and flung the saddle blanket over his back. The big horse quivered, but calmed, only sagging his back a little at the weight of the saddle. Beneteau mounted and spurred the big mount to a lope, but they avoided the road leading north and went into the hills, instead.

He rode straight until he hit the creek that their camp was on, then he pointed Bronc west and kept the big horse moving.

Beneteau didn't like the timing at all. He sensed trouble. He could always feel it in an uneasy way. Damn, those two white men were persistent. The creek wound through the bottom land, slowing them more than Beneteau realized. A pair of mallard ducks beat their wings frantically to rise through steam on the water and escape ahead of him. Beneteau pulled Bronc up to eye a bulky dark spot moving ahead on the flat edge of a meadow. It could be a crouching man. Another form moved. His hand slid toward the flap sealing the Henry. Then, a length of black rose from the shape and Beneteau relaxed. The objects were a pair of feeding Canada geese. They, too, rose at the approach of the rider and his horse. He was thinking darkly that the birds' flight was a foreboding warning when he cut away from the creek and headed to higher ground to scout ahead.

He rode Bronc to a clump of brush nestled on a hillside, dismounted and tied the horse before walking slowly to the brow of the hill from which he peered down. A half-mile away, he could see Horace Throckmorton Bunny III squatting at the campfire. Buster was downstream exploring the creek bank. Two riders approached from the south. Beneteau watched.

The raccoon scrambled up a stunted ash tree. It wrestled its way out on a branch overhanging the water and the flow of the stream over a narrow beaver dam must have interfered with its keen hearing.

Beneteau saw the riders pull up and one man extend his right arm with a revolver in it. The man's hand jumped. Buster plunged from his perch a split second before the report from the gun reached Beneteau's ears.

Beneteau's throat groaned. Gloom swirled over him like a great, grey mist. He would kill that bastard. Horace Throckmorton Bunny III caught his attention.

The shaman, who had been bent over the campfire, straightened and hobbled up from the base of a cut bank to the flat above to see what the commotion was.

The riders saw his scrawny form when it bobbed into view. They spurred their horses forward to him.

"What's all the shooting about?" Horace said when the men approached.

"Who wants to know?" said Cal.

"I am an ordained Baptist minister, sent by my teachers to preach the Gospel and convert sinners among the red men," Horace said in perfect English.

"Looks like just another damned Indian to me," said the other man.

"My friend here just potshot a coon hanging in a tree around the bend. But he fell in the water and didn't come up. We could have used some fresh meat."

"Bless you gentlemen. You are doing the Lord's work. He commanded human beings to take dominion over all living things."

"Jesus Christ, Cal, did you ever expect this? A damned sermon out in the middle of nowhere."

The man called Cal looked hard before he spoke. "We're trailing a half breed riding a piebald horse. Seen him?"

Horace scratched his back side before answering. He squinted south at the trail the men had used. "A description of a man's horse isn't much evidence to use in determining what one has seen, or not seen."

"You'd recognize this buzzard," the dark man said. "He looks closer to a white man. 'Bout my height, but slender. Nasty cuss. Breeds are no damned good. This one would steal the cloak off your back."

"I am a poor preacher," Horace said. "I doubt if anyone could be so lowly as to steal from the likes of me. Gentlemen, you could join me for a bite to eat if you'd like."

"Is that right," the dark man said. "What do you suppose an old coot like this is having for breakfast, Cal?"

"I was commanded to live from the land like John the Baptist," the old man said. "I was about to hunt for a fat rattlesnake before you happened upon me."

"Good god, Blackie. Do you suppose this minister might have a plate of grasshoppers too, as a side dish for that snake? Let's get out of here."

"May the Almighty have mercy on your souls and show you the light," the shaman said, shading his eyes with a bony hand while he watched the two ride past him to the north. "You wouldn't mind if I looked for that fat coon you shot?"

"Be our guest," Cal said. The two men rode away, laughing coarsely.

Phillipe Beneteau had restrained himself out of fear for the old man's life. He watched them ride over the horizon. By the time he and Bronc arrived at the creek, Horace Throckmorton Bunny III was tangled in the brush overhanging the flowing water. Beneteau could hear the old man muttering.

"Dratted creature. Come here. Where is your master? How am I supposed to help you, just sitting there staring? And stop that whining. My world would have been more dear if you had died."

Beneteau heard the other sound, too. The low whelping sounded like a puppy begging for its mother." He dismounted and ran to where the old man was and wiggled through the brush to his side.

"Mr. Beneteau, am I happy to see you. Your dratted friend is holed up in that creek bank."

Beneteau saw Buster's masked face. The raccoon was on its side, a streak of crimson leaking from a shoulder. Beneteau threw off his boots and clothes and dove into the water. He swam quickly to the animal and slowly gathered him in his arms. Buster trilled weakly.

"C'mon, pardner, you can make it. We'll have you fixed up in no time." Between the two of them, the old one tugging to pull Beneteau out of the water and Beneteau clutching the soggy raccoon, they managed to get back on the bank. Buster had been hit in the shoulder. The shaman made a mud pack for it.

Dressed and back at the camp with the fire going, Beneteau piled back on Bronc and rode off northwesterly before cutting back to pick up the trail of his two pursuers. He couldn't find it so he returned to camp.

Chapter 6

The greyness overhead thickened into sleet by the time Beneteau returned to camp. The old man huddled near the still form of Buster in a lean–to.

Beneteau said nothing when he dismounted and unbridled the piebald. He staked and tied the horse at its halter, then strode wearily to the sputtering fire.

“How is he?” he said, crumpling beside the old man and the animal.

“I am afraid I have bad news,” the old one said. “Your little friend is dead.”

Beneteau’s slim right hand shook when it touched the little animal. His hard eyes misted over before he buried his face in his arms.

The old man laid his arm on Beneteau’s shoulder. There was nothing he could say. The sleet rattled against the lean-to’s walls.

Beneteau's mind drifted back to the day three years earlier when he had been sitting at the edge of a beaver dam on a spring–fed creek in the Turtles. He was daydreaming with his eyes fixed on the opposing bank where he noticed the stems of tall grass waver. The grass wiggled along a meandering path until his curiosity moved him. He rose and crossed the creek on the ridge of the dam, then stopped ahead of the bending grass. He smiled when a black, wet nose appeared near the sole of one of his boots, then a black–masked face and at the end of the furry body trailed a ringed tail. The man reached down to touch the little critter and it shrank into a ball and hissed at him. Beneteau took a piece of jerky from his shirt pocket and dropped it in front of the raccoon's nose. The baby ignored the offering, but the scent drew him to the meat. Beneteau watched the little animal place its forepaws on the food and knead it back and forth before drawing it to his mouth. By the time the animal had eaten its fill, Beneteau had managed to slide his hand under its belly and raise it to his chest where it issued a couple of puppy–like whimpers and relaxed. That was how their friendship had begun. They had grown inseparable. The man figured the little one had lost its mother.

Beneteau heard the old man humming a death song, tapping with a digging stick on a rotted chunk of cottonwood. The thumping echoed in his mind and touched something deep within himself. It was like an ancient mystery revealed, the spirits of his ancestors coming forth with the beat to console him. The wind moaned in the sleet, the lean–to covering shuddered. Beneteau shook off the mood and reminded himself that he was grieving for an animal, a four–legged. One part of him said the creature was almost inanimate, but the deeper side of his nature told him he had lost a friend, his best, a genuine piece of himself and a part of the great Mystery of life. Beneteau's head sagged to his chest and he slept.

He sat through the night without toppling, a sign to Horace Throckmorton Bunny III of Beneteau's sadness at the passing of his animal friend. Beneteau stiffened almost as one who had died. The old one watched in silence when his companion stirred at daylight. The younger man's hazel eyes opened slowly and scanned the campsite. Buster no longer lay in front of him, but Beneteau noticed a small scaffold had been built at the brow of a nearby ridge. It was silhouetted by the sun.

"Thank you," Beneteau said to the old one.

The old man was about the business of fixing up some beans. The air was cleaned of dust by the moisture and morning light revealed a greenness in the refreshed creek–bank grasses.

"In my travels I have learned that Indians from India, a great land across the sea, purify their departed on a funeral bier," he said.

Beneteau wiped the sleep from his eyes before answering. "What the hell is a funeral bier?"

"That," the old man said, nodding toward the scaffold, "is a bier. It is purified by fire."

With anguish seeping back into him as he awoke, Beneteau thought somehow fire might release him from his sorrow.

The old man pulled a fat chunk of cottonwood from the fire and held it forth to Beneteau. When the younger man did not reach for it, he said firmly, "Come."

Beneteau followed the old man in his flowing, tattered cloak. The fire brand bobbed on either side of the old one's frail body. The scaffold was scaled down to the animal's size, the body fully enclosed in brush the old man had cut and gathered.

They stopped at the bier. Beneteau declined the old one's request that he fire the body.

"Great Creator, who has made all things for your children, who has given us the leaves and trees and all green things and their fruits, who has given us the four–leggeds for sustenance and companionship, who has given us fire to aid and to purify, please now accept back this small creature in renewal. Comfort his friend who remains behind after the little creature's short earthly journey, and remind the man that this little four–legged has only moved into the realm of the other side and is really with him yet in the journey the man continues."

He touched the brush at a corner and the flames spread quickly, their dancing orange colors pulsating against the backdrop of the rising sun, whose pink glow spread on the horizon.

Beneteau's mind leapt from the death scene forward to an imagined encounter with the dark man who had shot Buster. "That bastard," he said, watching the black smoke rise and dissipate. The two mourners retreated back from the ridge to eat and break camp.

Beneteau knew the Mandans were camped somewhere along the Missouri River ahead. When he offered his foot to the old man to use to get on behind him on Bronc, he intended to take the Medicine Man to his people.

They rode 20 miles before they came to the Knife River.

"Might your people be camped downstream?" he said. Bronc sighed as they dismounted and when Beneteau loosened the cinch the rangy piebald shook himself.

Mr. Beneteau, "I have no idea where my tribal people are," the Medicine Man said. "All people are my flock to be tended."

"If I was in your position, I'd be thinking about getting with some of my kin."

"For now, White Owl—I like what the Sioux call you a lot—you are my kin. We are all brothers."

"Hear that, Bronc," Beneteau said to his horse who nibbled tufts of grass growing on the river bank. "We got us a new brother."

The old man poked with his digging stick for wild onions. "Lets get a pot of beans going. We'll feel better. God Almighty wants his children to be happy on this earth."

"If He wants to make me happy, He'll help us get a little meat. I'll walk that ridge. Old Bronc needs a rest," Beneteau said, drawing the Henry from its scabbard, then removing the saddle. He felt like he needed a rest, too, away from Horace's prattle. Bronc had grown sluggish under the constant double load, even though the old man was a bundle of skin and bones. How the hell could a man have an appetite like a bear and stay as skinny as a jay bird?

When he flushed a spirited jackrabbit, Beneteau let go his high, screeching whistle. The big rabbit halted its bounding, running escape and sat on its haunches, big ears trying to tune in the direction of the sound. The Henry cracked and Beneteau retrieved the game.

The rabbit's ears felt warm between his fingers. Beneteau was enjoying the thought of getting a taste of fresh meat when he spied a rustling of leaves in a thicket below him on the creek bank.

The rabbit thumped dully as it hit the ground below him, the sound creating a weird harmony with the sharp crack of the Henry being cocked.

His eyes riveted on the spot, then swept left and right for further movement before Beneteau crouched and advanced. The rifle was at eye level and pressed tightly against his shoulder with his finger pulling the trigger when the black object in the brush flicked itself and another object joined it. A pair of mule ears emerged.

Beneteau dropped prone on the prairie behind a chunk of pink granite left embedded in the grass by a melting glacier of long ago.

"You, in there," he said, firmly. "Show yourself."

The mule's ears twitched in his direction, but nothing more.

The old man, watching from below and off to his right, shouted, "Mr. Beneteau, what on earth are you doing?"

Beneteau waved the Medicine Man to silence, but the old man ignored him and hobbled up the hill.

"Damn it, would you get down and stay down? There's a bushwhacker in that thicket."

But Horace Throckmorton Bunny III kept coming and the mule managed to wiggle its nose through the branches to peer at Beneteau with its dark eyes.

Beneteau expected a shot and to see the old man topple. Instead, the old one stood over him, bent at the waist, his right hand raised to shield his eyes.

"Why are you hiding from that mule, Hinhanska?"

Beneteau rose and uncocked the hammer on his rifle. The two men advanced to the animal. It brayed a loud welcome causing the Henry to rise sharply to Beneteau's shoulder again.

"There, there now, long–eared friend, we haven't come to cause you harm," said the Medicine Man.

When they entered the thicket, it was apparent the mule was tethered to a sapling. The campfire was cold. A bedroll was laid out, but the lump in it was still. Beneteau, strung taut, noticed a human hand reaching from the head side of the bedroll, the pale fingers clutching a tuft of brown wrapping paper. Beneteau poked the form with the tip of his rifle. The body was stiff. The old man reached down and touched the outstretched hand. He knelt and slowly peeled the wool blanket back revealing a balding head with long, stringy black and grey hair, a lock of which had spread over the exposed side of the man's ashen face.

"He's very dead," said Beneteau. "What's on the paper?"

"Hinhanska, show some respect," the old one said.

"Respect hell. He's dead."

"He's watching from the spirit world. When a human leaves this earth with his eyes open, he can never rest. Show some reverence, lower your voice."

Horace Throckmorton Bunny III pressed two fingers of his right hand against one of the man's open eyelids and closed it. Then, he cradled the man's head with his hand and did the same for the other eye using his left hand.

"We must make him a final resting place in the white man's style."

Beneteau snatched up the piece of wrapping paper and scrutinized it.

"What does it mean?" he said, handing the paper to the old man.

"Heh, you can't read, can you, Hinhanska? You can always tell a man who can't read. He moves fast like a shallow stream."

"Another sermon, another damned sermon. Can you do anything without preaching?"

"It is my calling. Come, help me carry him to that buffalo wallow we passed. We will cave it in around his body and cover the grave with stones and make a little marker. Then, I will tell you what the paper says."

They rolled the body on the blanket. The old man could barely keep his end from bouncing on the ground and Beneteau could hear the dead man's boots scrape hollowly on the hard prairie. When they got the corpse to the hole, Beneteau caved its small banks at the edges and dirt lumps rolled to the blanket. Horace had squatted and was singing again. He paused as the dust from Beneteau's work began to settle.

"Now a few stones and we will be finished," he said to Beneteau, then he renewed his chant.

With the body stowed safely in the bosom of Mother Earth, Beneteau untied the mule and led it to the creek for a drink. There was no saddle and no bridle in the small camp, only a small crudely fashioned pack. Beneteau undid the halter rope at its ring and fastened it to separate sides of the worn leather to form reins. Copper rivets holding the contraption together left streaks of green mold along its musty straps.

"Well let's see what you can do," he said, swinging quickly onto the animal's back. "Let's go," He raked the animal's sides with his boot heels. Nothing happened. He threw his right leg over the mule's back and slid off. "Stubborn bastard," he mumbled.

The old man looked up from the paper when Beneteau approached after tying the animal back to the sapling.

"This is the man's last will and testament."

"Great," said Beneteau. "And what does it say?"

"To whoever finds me, my earthly belongings are yers. Ned Thompson, Iowa."

"Looks like me and you get to split an old mule," Beneteau said. "And it ain't even broke to ride. Can you imagine an old geezer like him roaming the hills with this critter?"

"He must have been a holy man," the Medicine Man said.

"I'd say he was a prospector."

Beneteau kicked at a mourning dove's carcass the prospector must have been fixing to eat before he died. The dead bird thumped on the ground. He retrieved it and pressed his thumbs and index fingers along its body, coming to a lump in its breast. Beneteau peeled the bird's breast from its back and opened the crop. The prospector had sewn the bird back together with string. Beneteau asked Horace Throckmorton Bunny III to hold out one of his bony hands, then dumped the contents of the crop. The gold nuggets that dropped varied from about the size of a ladybug to ant eggs. There was an ounce or two. Neither man had any idea what the nuggets were worth.

"Now, you see, Hinhanska, the Great Spirit has already rewarded us for doing what was right."

"Okay, but I'll hang onto the gold and you hang onto the mule. Get on him. I've got a rabbit laying back on the hill and I'm ready for some grub." He boosted Horace to the animal's back and led the mule out of the thicket. He stowed the gold nuggets back in the bird's crop and tucked it in his shirt pocket.

The mule followed wherever he went, so he tossed the lead rope back to the Medicine Man. "Hang on," he said, breaking into a jog, and the mule trotted right behind. Horace Throckmorton Bunny III didn't seem to know near as much about sitting on a mule as he did about everything else. Beneteau slowed to a walk before the old man toppled off the mule's back from the bone–jarring gait.

"The Great Spirit makes each day a new trial," Horace said, breathing heavily.

In the middle of polishing off the roast rabbit, Beneteau sighted two riders crawling on the ridge line two miles away. He saddled Bronc and told the Medicine Man he would move off to a clump of buffalo berry bushes as a guard until they learned who the riders were.

The pair approached the camp on good horses, which danced sideways, straining against the reins to be loosed. By the time the two men arrived and were talking to the old man,

Beneteau had his feather up in his hat, his moccasins back on and he let out a whoop as he turned Bronc loose to full stride. Beneteau swung his right leg over the saddle and hung an instant at Bronc's side before he touched his feet to the ground and swung upward in an arch before coming down on the horse's other side and rising back again to the saddle. He gave his half–breed tribesmen their buffalo runner's salute.

He slid the piebald in a cloud of dust and jumped to the ground where the three men hugged warmly before Beneteau managed to introduce his old companion.

"Jean Baptiste, Petit Jacques, my traveling partner and holy man Horace Throckmorton Bunny III. He's a Mandan who spent a lot of time living with white people."

"I hope you are not as difficult to civilize as Mr. Beneteau," the old man said.

"What brings you this way?" Beneteau said.

"We were visiting the Assiniboines west along the Missouri to set up a trading time and to locate a big buffalo herd," said Ti Jacques, whose build bore a similarity to Beneteau's. His father was known as Gros Jacques, but was actually shorter than his son. "We got a little crazy and decided to drop down this way on a hunch you might be coming home by now."

"You figured I might have struck it rich."

"No," said Jean Baptiste, "Phillipe, you will never be rich either. You will just be poor like the rest of us. It is our destiny. To ride like the wind, hunt the buffalo and sleep with our beautiful women. Oops, sorry padre."

"Don't forget we are the best traders in the land," said Ti Jacques.

"You are a boastful lot," said Mr. Bunny. "Pride comes before a fall."

The Métis brought out their coffee and a beat up tin pot and they gathered around the smoldering campfire. Beneteau offered them the remains of the rabbit and volunteered to hunt for deer. But Jean Baptiste withdrew strips of buffalo jerky from his saddlebag. With Horace's left–over beans, the new arrivals enjoyed a hearty prairie meal. While they were catching up on the news over their third pot of coffee, Beneteau reached in his shirt pocket then chucked the bird crop on the ground. It dented the powdery dirt when it hit.

"What's in there—lead?" said Ti Jacques.

Jean Baptiste picked up the crop and undid the rawhide thong Beneteau used to tie the small sack.

"You have struck gold," Jean Baptiste said, rolling the nuggets across one of his huge palms. Beneteau told the story about the miner. They agreed the miner probably had found his gold in the Black Hills. They were ready to go look for some, too. Beneteau took their minds off the subject by promising a party when they got the Medicine Man back to his people and could locate a trader with a supply of whiskey. Beneteau knew none of them had time to look for gold. The people were waiting for their reports for the buffalo hunt. It would be no time before winter.

"The evils of gold and whiskey have ruined many," Horace said. "I hope and pray for your sakes that you keep your word to your people."

"You worry too much," Beneteau said. "But you are part of us until you leave. And we Métis have never forced any man to drink whiskey or chase women and buffalo. Let's get moving," he told the others.

On the trail again, the Métis rode their spirited horses expertly and Horace Throckmorton Bunny III followed behind Beneteau on the mule. The old man called the mule, "Opportunity." Said he had learned from white people, that the world was full of opportunity. They had so much of it that they were always willing to give anyone an opportunity and that deceased miner had given him an Opportunity to learn to ride.

The mule must have been part of a pack string at one time because it just kept its nose following along behind Bronc. The old man nearly fell off when the mule felt uncomfortable at being followed by one of the other horses. Its black legs raised off the ground and lashed back at whatever was behind. Horace thought it was trying to buck him off, but the Métis just grinned and told him to hang on. They liked the Medicine Man's grit.

The riders came to a large expanse of flat Knife River bottom land. Their horses were rested and pranced.

"To the tree for the first bite of the next fresh deer liver," Beneteau said. Bronc's haunches dropped and his muscles rippled in the sunlight under his dark hide as he launched himself into the wind. Beneteau leaned low over the saddle and felt the saddle horn dance against his midriff. He looked left and right under his hat brim. Jean Baptiste wore a serious expression, Ti Jacques a wide grin. Their horses' manes and tails swirled in the air gushing past. The animals seemed to have shrunk in height and grown in length as they clawed their way across the flat toward the gnarled tree hanging at the river bank.

Opportunity broke with the horses, but only trotted stiffly until her rider was unseated, then she coasted into a gentle rocking gallop. No one heard Horace shouting, "You must be mad!"

Beneteau responded to the racing yips of his friends by yipping back at them. They were like a pack of coyotes doing the job for which God created them.

There was no clear cut winner as the buffalo runners' noses crossed the imaginary finish line. The men knew that a half-mile race was not a real test for their long–winded mounts.

“The first taste of the deer’s liver is reserved for Mr. Bunny,” said Jean Baptiste who reined in his big sorrel and returned to the group.

“The honor is his,” agreed Ti Jacques, laughing.

“Here comes his mule,” said Beneteau. “I better get on back there and give him a hand.”

Beneteau loped the piebald back to the figure whose cloak beat against his frail frame.

“You are mad,” the old man said when Beneteau got within earshot.

“You better learn to hang to that mule, or you’ll be afoot again,” Beneteau said. “How can a Mandan get bucked off by a mule?”

“I was taken in by missionaries when I was quite young,” the Medicine Man replied. He shaded his eyes with his right hand and held out his left for Beneteau to grasp.

Beneteau reached for him, but the second their skin touched, the old man’s bony fingers clasped with surprising strength on his wrist. The old one’s other hand grabbed Beneteau’s extended forearm. Horace Throckmorton Bunny III dipped his body and lifted Beneteau from Bronc’s back, the smooth action depositing Beneteau in a heap on the ground.

Grunting and cursing, Beneteau rolled to his feet to face the old man, who stood with his Derringers cocked and aimed at the younger man’s head.

“Manners, Mr. Beneteau. You have absolutely no manners, no respect for your elders.”

“You old coot. You treacherous old coot.”

“Easy now, Mr. Beneteau. One of these darn things might go off.”

"I came back to give you a ride."

"No, you came back because the Creator likes you and wanted you to learn a new lesson."

"You're crazy."

"Maybe, but as you can see, I have you at a disadvantage. Crazy would be for you to not see the severity of this situation."

"Okay, okay. What is it the Creator wants me to know?"

"He wants you to know, Hinhanska, that I have been joined with you to aid you, but not to be made the fool by you."

"We were just having a little fun. How can you take falling off a mule so serious?"

"Manners, Mr. Beneteau."

"All right. I am sorry. We Métis think riding is easy for everyone."

"Opportunity is the first four–legged critter that has ever had me on its back alone," the old one said. "I was just beginning to enjoy it a little bit when you and your ill–mannered tribesmen ruined my day."

"C'mon, Mr. Bunny, let's be friends again," said Beneteau stretching forth his hands for a lift.

"You are young enough to get up by yourself," the old man said, tucking the Derringers away beneath his robe.

Shortly, both were astride Bronc and loping toward the waiting forms of Ti Jacques and Jean Baptiste.

Chapter 7

They camped early by a spring found seeping from a hill-side.

"We won't be the only ones who are smart enough to use this water," Beneteau said.

"A remarkable observation, Hinhanska," said Horace. "I'll get some water boiling if you Métis boys can gather some firewood. It should be dry but you know that, I am sure."

"Ti Jacques, catch the top of that hill," said Beneteau, who slipped into a position of leadership. "Jean Baptiste and I will get some wood for our holy cook."

"Aw crap, Phillipe," said the big man, "you gonna stick me with women's work?"

"You could be cook," Beneteau said.

Horace, ignoring them, had put his digging stick to work gouging a hole for the fire. "And bring in some rocks to line this fire hole," he said without looking at the two men.

Ti Jacques was just a dark bump at the top of the spring-fed hill. He waved all clear.

Jean Baptiste and Beneteau staked the animals, then ambled down the hillside on either side of a gully that led to flat land strewn with small granite rocks, but no wood, just dried piles of buffalo chips.

"Why do we have to have a fire anyway?" said Jean Baptiste.

"The old one has real coffee tucked in that shoulder bag and I've grown fond of his beans," Beneteau said. "Besides, we need a little foot exercise."

"Watch it, Phillipe," Jean Baptiste warned. "I hear a rattler in them rocks." The big half–breed knew that his friend, blessed with many talents though he was, was tone deaf to a rattlesnake's warning.

"Bark if you see him," Beneteau replied.

"Bark hell, I'll be jumping into a cloud," Jean Baptiste said. "There he is."

The snake was about three–feet long and slithering out of the prairie grass away from them toward a rock pile bunched up in the gully.

Phillipe Beneteau sprinted toward the creature and before it could recover speared it with his right hand by the back of head.

"You crazy bastard," Jean Baptiste said.

The snake hung in the air, writhing, fangs bared and glaring at his captors.

"He's rattlin' and spitting mad," said Jean Baptiste. "Can't you hear him, Phillipe?"

"Can't hear a thing," said Beneteau. "But let's see if our padre will make us some snake stew."

“Holy Mother, you ain’t gonna pull that old bedroll trick on him, Phillipe.”

“Coil him inside it? Nah, you already know what that’s like. Let’s just see how that smart, old coot handles snake meat.” He snapped the snake like a whip and broke its neck.

They toted as many round stones and chips as they could back to the campsite.

Horace Throckmorton Bunny III was still too busy to look up when they arrived. Beneteau, cradling fuel in his left arm, was holding the crawling critter behind his back with his right.

“Just put your stones and wood by that hole,” the old man told them.

Jean Baptiste dropped the rocks. While Horace busied himself with dumping beans in his pot and tossing in a few pinches of salt and whatever else he had in his seasoning bag, Beneteau arranged the snake in a coil and laid it by the dung in the grass at the edge of the fire hole.

The Medicine Man left his prairie kitchen to tend to making a fire while the two Métis flung themselves prone on the ground against their bedrolls and watched.

His robe flowing behind him, Horace stooped to pick up a rock and lay it neatly on the wall of the hole. The next stone was his undoing. Beneteau had placed the snake with its head back as if ready to strike.

Horace froze when he saw it. “Mr. Beneteau,” he said softly, “there is a rattlesnake right in front of my face.”

“What?” Beneteau said.

“A rattlesnake, Mr. Beneteau. I dar’nt move.”

“You are supposed to be out of there by now,” said Beneteau. “Where on earth did you learn to not move?”

"It is written in every story I've read about snakes," whispered Horace. "Freeze, don't move."

"Hang on, Mr. Bunny, I'll try to pick him off."

"Please do, but be careful," said Horace from the side of his mouth, teeth clenched. "I have much good work to do before I die."

Beneteau grabbed the Henry, cocked it and edged closer to the frightened old man. "Where is he?"

He's just to the right in front of my forehead," said Horace.

"If I shoot, I may hit you."

"For God's sake, do something," said the holy man.

Beneteau laid his free hand on the old man's back, the rifle barrel beside his head and told him to be steady.

"What are you going to do?" said Horace.

"Be very still," Beneteau said. And he slid his hand slowly along the old man's back, then along his neck and up through his long grey mane to where the hair thinned. His slim fingers slipped over the edge of Horace's forehead, past his eyes and tip–toed down his nose. He released the hammer on the Henry just as his left hand darted from the tip of Horace's nose to the head of the snake and he grabbed it right by the throat.

Horace came erect and stared. Beneteau tossed the snake in the air and caught it around his neck and there it hung limp as a rag.

"Do you think you could cook this critter?" said Beneteau, grinning widely.

"You scurvy garbage pit," the old man said. "The snake is dead."

"You don't think us Métis boys would allow a snake to come into our camp and kill the cook, do you?"

Jean Baptiste turned his face to the ground and shook with laughter.

"Take that snake and get out of my sight," Horace said. "I can't believe you would be so unprincipled. You are worse than a snake in the grass yourself."

"Aw, Mr. Bunny, Phillipe was just having a little fun. He's done something like that to all of us," Jean Baptiste said.

Fun, eh?" said Horace. "An old Chinese cook I read about in a western magazine told some uncivilized cowboys playing pranks on him, *'You quit playing tricks on Chang, he stop peeing in your coffee.'*"

"Aw gees," Jean Baptiste said, "you wouldn't pull a lowdown stunt like that on us boys, would you?"

"I would sleep with one eye open," said Horace.

"We do," said Beneteau.

The snake was still writhing with muscle spasms in the grass where Beneteau had dropped it when the sun bowed beneath the horizon.

After chowing down on Horace's beans, Beneteau left the campfire to relieve Ti Jacques for supper and to take the first watch under the emerging stars.

"What's for supper?" Ti Jacques said when he approached.

"Thousands of things," said Beneteau.

"Just beans?"

"Yeh, the old man wouldn't cook rattlesnake."

"Was that what all that arm waving was about? I'm happy he doesn't like snake."

"I guess so," said Beneteau. "I believe I hurt his feelings by bringing it into camp. See anything?"

"Nah, only a little dust off to the northwest. You still worrying about that posse, Phillipe?"

"Not anymore than I worry about all those cattle coming into this country. There's not enough grass here for both cattle and buffalo."

"The buffalo will be here forever," Ti Jacques said. "They're built for this country."

"I wouldn't be too sure," said Beneteau. "This year of '83 could be our last hunt."

"Then what will we be?" said Ti Jacques. "We are the people who live in two worlds. No buffalo, no trade, no Métis."

"I don't know," said Beneteau. "But you better get some grub and sleep." Beneteau lay prone at the brow of the hill, the Henry by his side. He watched Ti Jacques glide toward the fire, then pondered his own words in the dark.

For 40 or more years, the Métis elders had worried that the buffalo herds were thinning. He had listened as a boy to their stories, of how his people moved out in wagon trains of up to 600 carts with women and children to take up the trail of the buffalo on the plains of Dakota Territory. They mostly had muskets in those days. They had problems then with the Sioux, but the full bloods had learned to respect the Métis as fighting men and top traders with the white men. After all, the Métis could see in both directions. They were expert horsemen, military strategists, used their two–wheeled wagons for transportation and their women were mostly dark–eyed and beautiful. The Métis didn't fit in well with either the white or red people, but they were welded to each other by their heritage. They loved the hunt, but those with the far sight worried that times were changing. Phillipe Beneteau thought he now saw the change coming up the trail with those cattle being driven by cowboys.

A faint metallic click in the darkness snapped him back to his job on the hilltop. Beneteau cradled the Henry and eased back the rifle's hammer as he peered toward the sound. Like a startled deer, all of his senses were riveted on that spot. A boot dislodged a rock below him and a man's voice cursed in a low tone. Beneteau fired three rapid shots at the sound. It was a signal to his fellow Métis that they were under attack. Beneteau rolled away from his position and came up just as the night air parted in flashes of gunfire below him. He fired the Henry at the flashes and rolled again. The glowing embers of the small campfire below him were doused. Beneteau could-n't be sure but he guessed the attackers were the posse men and they must have picked up their trail. He heard muffled voices now, not 100 yards from where he lay.

"Spread out and surround the bastard," a raspy voice said.

Beneteau hooted," Uh-uh-oh, uh-uh-oh, uh-uh-oh," like a great-horned owl. Ti Jacques and Jean Baptiste knew now that they could charge the attackers' flanks. Their horses' hoof beats pounded behind him as they rounded the hill on both his right and left in the blackness. The Henry barked rapidly and drew again the flashes of the attackers' guns. He watched for a moment as Ti Jacques and Jean Baptiste opened up on the posse men. His tribesmen would cross paths and regroup with him at the campsite. Beneteau came up crouched and running hard. When he tumbled into camp, Horace Throckmorton Bunny III held Bronc and the mule.

"Let him free, Mr. Bunny, and get up with me," Beneteau ordered. If he wants to come with us, he can keep up on his own." They both mounted the piebald and waited in the dark for the two returning Métis, then they set off at a full gallop away from the campsite. If Beneteau had wanted, they would have defended their position.

They rode in silence until Beneteau called a rest stop.

"Anybody hurt?" he said. No one was but within seconds, the Métis had their rifles out and cocked for action at the sound of approaching horse hooves.

"Hold it," Beneteau said before anyone could fire. The galloping hoof beats led right into their midst. "It's Opportunity," Beneteau said. "Let's keep going." And they set off at a trot, stopping occasionally to listen, but only the hoof beats of the mule followed in the night.

"Who are they, Phillipe?" Jean Baptiste said.

"They are the same bunch that has been trailing me since Deadwood. I heard their leader's raspy voice. He hates us breeds, but he has left me with the idea he don't like much of anything. I'd like to see how he fights when the odds are even."

They pushed hard in the night with their eyes fixed on the Big Dipper's North Star, always veering to the northeast toward the next big settlement, Devils Lake. As dawn broke, they could see the Missouri River bending before them.

The wind kicked up as Beneteau called another halt in a patch of brush. He sent Ti Jacques to check their back trail while they munched jerky.

"Mr. Beneteau," said Horace, "you certainly have a way of making my life more interesting."

"Won't be long now and you ought to be back with your people," Beneteau said. "And after we get past Devils Lake, we'll be closer to being with ours."

Ti Jacques jogged down to report there was nothing following except that mule.

"We'll wait for him a bit, then get Mr. Bunny mounted again," said Beneteau.

"Hinhanska, your white blood is showing. You want to give me the old Opportunity."

"No offense, Mr. Bunny, but Bronc could use a breather."

While they waited, Beneteau withdrew the dove crop and dumped the gold in his hand, then showed it to his two tribesmen again.

"We'll use this for supplies in Devils Lake," he said.

"Gees, Phillipe, I really never seen gold before, Jean Baptiste said."

"Don't get greedy for it and you'll live longer," Beneteau said.

"You sound like Koohkoum Emma," Jean Baptiste said.

Ti Jacques said he had to find some pig weed leaves and visit Mother Nature. Said his stomach kind of bothered him.

"Let's don't get caught out here with our pants down," said Beneteau. He thought maybe it was the excitement they had just come through, but he was feeling a little loose himself.

"Phillipe, I think I better join Ti Jacques," Jean Baptiste said and he disappeared around the hillside.

"Wonder what got into those boys?" Beneteau said.

Horace Throckmorton Bunny III was stroking the mule and fashioning a pannier to carry his tote bag and only other earthly possession, his tattered blanket. He was humming Rock of Ages.

"Boy, did I get cleaned out," Ti Jacques said when he got back. "That's the first time Jean Baptiste and I have sat side by side since we drank from an alkali mud hole."

Beneteau told him to keep an eye on the southwest for any approaching riders, then excused himself, complaining that his stomach was knotting up.

"Boy, Mr. Bunny," he said to the old man when Beneteau was gone, "I sure was glad you didn't cook that rattlesnake last night."

"Yes," Horace replied, "just the thought of it makes me sick to my stomach. Of course, if I felt that bad I'd just have a pinch of these Epson salts," he said, dangling a tobacco sack from his bony fingers. "They'd clean out the poisons in no time." He pushed the sack back in his tote bag.

When the other two men returned from doing their business, Beneteau was first to speak.

"It's amazing how we three got sour stomachs but you, Mr. Bunny, seem fit as a young bull."

"The Lord is, indeed, a mysterious worker," Horace said. "He has given man all things of the earth to use for his pleasure or displeasure."

"I think Mr. Bunny is trying to tell us what Koohkoum used to say, 'Watch out what you do in life, 'cause things have a way of coming back on you, '" Ti Jacques said.

"We better move on," said Beneteau. "We've got to cross that river before dark. You and Opportunity going to be able to make it?" he said to Horace.

"Oh, we're feeling fine," the old man said. "And you, Mr. Beneteau?"

"I'm learning all the time," said Beneteau. "You can catch a snake and scare the cook but you'll pay for it in the end."

"Hind end," said Jean Baptiste."

"I'll drink to that," said Ti Jacques.

"Smart men," said Horace Throckmorton Bunny III.

They struck out for the wide river glimmering like a silver ribbon before them.

The Métis knew there was a barge crossing on the river somewhere. But the main trail bordered the river, so they weren't sure where they'd find it. Beneteau called for a count of their money to see if they had to work their way across cutting wood for steamers the ferry barge owner could sell, or if they could buy a ride.

"We could use the gold, Phillipe," Ti Jacques suggested when they pooled their resources and came up $4 short of the usual $5 fee.

"The last thing we want is for any of these greedy settlers to know we've got gold," Beneteau said. "I say we spread out and locate the crossing. We'll work our way across." He sent Ti Jacques north and Jean Baptiste south. "Keep an eye open for Mandans," he told them. "We'd hate to have to turn Mr. Bunny loose on his own to find his people with just his mule and his good book."

"Where do you want to meet?" said Ti Jacques.

"Mr. Bunny and I will keep heading straight and you can follow the river back to the big bend. I'll watch our back trail from the tree line. Remember, boys, no drinking. We'll have our backs to the river."

By mid morn, Beneteau had scouted the river's bend and Jean Baptiste had returned with no news. Horace had started a fire and was making coffee.

"Mr. Beneteau," he said when the two men sauntered into camp after staking their horses, "there hasn't been a soul coming out of those hills since we passed through."

"No sign of Ti Jacques?" Beneteau said.

"You're the only living beings I've seen all morning," said Horace Throckmorton Bunny III. His Bible lay on a fallen cottonwood, the pages held open by a branch of grey driftwood. He paused to read in it between stirring his beans and poking the fire.

"That your cook book, Mr. Bunny?" said Jean Baptiste.

"It has recipes for life," said Horace.

"Right now, I'd settle for some coffee," said Beneteau. "We'd best get some grub and find Ti Jacques."

"And the crossing," said Jean Baptiste.

"You boys would be better off if you found the Lord first," said Horace.

"We'll get all the preaching we need from Father Belgarde when we get home," said Beneteau. "Let's have some of that coffee. And no more funny stuff, if you don't mind."

"Just remember Chang," Horace said. He picked up his Bible, squinted at his pages and added, "And Solomon says in Proverbs, 'For a just man falleth seven times, and riseth up again; but the wicked shall fall into mischief.'"

The three men mounted and winded their way through a river–bottom forest of tall cottonwoods on their way upriver in search of Ti Jacques. Rounding a bend, they spied a ferry barge moored to a huge chunk of driftwood on the bank. Beneteau said he would ride down and check out tents pitched near a cedar–pole corral.

Aside from his ponytail, he looked like a drifting cowhand as he entered the camp perimeter.

"Mornin'," he said nodding to a family huddled around a camp fire. Two small children, still in nightshirts, gawked out from the legs of their mother as he passed by. The woman didn't look up, but her man, nodded to return the greeting.

Beneteau aimed the piebald at a tent from which loud voices emanated. The closer he got convinced him the men inside were drinking.

"I won fair," he heard the voice of Ti Jacques proclaim loudly. Before Beneteau could dismount, a clamor arose in the tent and the wiry Métis came pitching outside, a big white man right on his tail.

Ti Jacques, struggling to get up from his knees, took a boot in the ribs before Beneteau leapt to the ground to intervene.

Despite his size, the big man was no match for Beneteau, who shoved him aside. His breath wreaked of alcohol.

"This breed may deserve a good whippin' from you," Beneteau told the man, "but he's my hired hand and I need him in one piece to do his work."

"Wal', you gist get his cheatin' little brown ass on outta here," the man said. He backed off before the steely look in Beneteau's eyes. He turned and staggered back into the tent.

Beneteau tugged Ti Jacques to his feet.

"Damn it, I told you no drinking, Ti Jacques."

"Geesh, Phillipe, I wash just tryin' to get shum money to crosh the big river." A couple of silver dollars clanked in his rawhide shirt pocket when Beneteau tried to steady him.

"C'mon, lets get you to your horse, " Beneteau said.

"Heesh over there by thet corral," said Ti Jacques.

Beneteau got his tribesman mounted and led his horse back to where Horace and Jean Baptiste were waiting in the trees overlooking the landing.

"Mr. Bunny," Beneteau said when they approached, "have you got anything in that bag to sober a man up? Might need a little doctoring, too. Ti Jacques took a pretty good kick in the ribs down there."

"Geesh, Phillipe, I feel fine," said Ti Jacques. "Why're you worrin' 'bout me?"

"I think Mr. Beneteau is worrying more about getting across that river than anything. You Métis boys don't seem to be able to stay out of trouble," Horace said. "I'm sure I have something that will help if I can get this mule to stand still."

Opportunity tugged at the rope reins and tried to get a mouthful of grass.

"I'll help you, Mr. Bunny," said Jean Baptiste. He grabbed the reins from the Medicine Man's hands, just in time to get nipped in the wrist by the mule. The bite drew blood. Jean Baptiste swore at the mule. The mule stepped on his foot.

"Hold on, you bastard, or I'll get a chunk of wood and clobber ya," Jean Baptiste said. Horace Throckmorton Bunny III was bobbing at the mule's side, trying to get in his tote bag.

Beneteau leapt to the ground to help out and the mule cut loose with both hind feet, narrowly missing his head. Ti Jacques fell off his horse and passed out.

"For crying out loud, hang on to that cuss," Beneteau shouted to Jean Baptiste. He snatched the bag from the mule's neck and handed it to Horace. Jean Baptiste was sucking his bleeding wrist and hopping on one foot.

"Let her have some slack, Jean Baptiste," Beneteau said. And when the big man loosened his grip, the mule settled down and munched at the grass.

"God, I don't know who is the bigger handful around here," Beneteau said.

Horace knelt beside Ti Jacques and felt his ribs. "I don't think anything is broken." he said.

While Horace was fishing in his bag, Beneteau opened Ti Jacques's shirt pocket and pulled out two silver dollars. He pocketed the money, figuring as he did they were just two dollars short of having enough to make it across the river.

Beneteau told Jean Baptiste to ride back a ways and see if they were being trailed. “Don’t tarry, just check it out and get back here as fast as you can.”

Beneteau left the Medicine Man to work out reviving and sobering his patient and he rode back down to where a group of men were gathering around the barge. They eyed him.

“Who’s the ramrod?” Beneteau said to the men.

“I’m Phil Benett,” he said, Anglicizing his real name. It worked wherever he went, even in Deadwood.

“What do you need?” said a balding man whose forehead was beaded in sweat. His muscular arms worked to square the barge to the river bank for loading.

“I have three hands besides myself, three horses and a mule,” Beneteau said.

“Be six bits each for the animals, two bits each for the human beings,” the barge man said. “We leave in half an hour. Usually cost more, but the river is still low and business has been slow, so I’m cutting my price to keep folks from fordin’ the damned river on sand bars. It’s dangerous.”

“We’ll be here,” Beneteau said, turning Bronc and loping back to the trees. Beneteau figured he couldn’t be too hard on Ti Jacques. He saved the day. He was kind of thirsty himself and gambling was in their Métis blood. But they were still a ways from home and being chased besides.

“Looks like we’re stuck with the Medicine Man,” he mused aloud. No time to find the Mandans. Beneteau wasn’t sure if the camp preacher even wanted to find his people.

Horace revived Ti Jacques and had him sipping a cup of herbal tea when Beneteau got back.

"You going to live, Ti Jacques?" Beneteau said. "'cause if you ain't, you're going to die in the saddle. Mount up, we're crossing the river."

"I'm sorry, Phillipe," Ti Jacques said. "I just had to get into that card game and those white men tried to get me drunk. Did I win anything? I thought I had a couple of dollars."

"You did okay," said Beneteau. "We'll owe the river crossing to you. Let's go."

When they got to the barge, they drew stares from everybody.

"Look at that scarecrow riding that donkey," one onlooker said.

"This, sir, is a mule," Horace Throckmorton Bunny III said. "You, sir, are an ass."

"Why you old crow bait, I ought to knock some sense into you."

"He's my camp cook," Beneteau said, intervening. "We call him Blabby. "But he can make the best baked beans I've ever tasted. You want a piece of him, you get a mouthful of me. We're just here to cross the river to get back to my ranch at Minot."

"You ought to teach him some manners," the man said.

"Can't teach him anymore than I can teach that mule," Beneteau said.

"I suppose the Indian works for beads," the white man said, laughing.

"Nah, I traded a blanket to some Arikara for him," Beneteau said. "Now, he owes me. He is a Mandan, but he's been to school and has book learning. Made him kind of sassy. If you really want him, I'd make you a good trade."

"Nope, I don't need no mouthy Indian hangin' with me. He's your problem, mister. But I'd teach him some manners, if he were mine."

Jean Baptiste and Ti Jacques said nothing but hoped with Beneteau that their padre would keep his mouth shut before they got in more trouble.

Beneteau led Bronc on the barge, and his tribesmen followed with their mounts. Opportunity balked.

Beneteau and Jean Baptiste hooked arms behind the mule's tail and Ti Jacques pulled on the reins.

"Your slave, Mr. Beneteau?" Horace said. "Odd that I, your slave, am watching you labor."

"For God's sake, Mr. Bunny, would you pipe down?" Beneteau said under his breath.

Opportunity finally gave in and leapt on the barge, nearly knocking Ti Jacques over the side.

The barge was midway in the crossing, when shouting erupted on the bank. Jean Baptiste said in a low voice that he had seen five riders gallop into the river–side camp. They sat horseback waving their arms at the barge.

"They'll just have to wait their turn," the barge man said. The muddy current lapped at the craft's sides as the barge was poled in the shallows and oared through the deeper water.

"There's the stuff that's dangerous," the barge man said to anyone within earshot. The boat rocked through a whirlpool, then steadied as the river flattened out.

When the barge came to rest on the other bank, Beneteau and his three companions walked their mounts off the loading plank. The barge man began loading for the return trip. And as soon as they were horseback and out of sight of the craft, they spurred their horses to a gallop.

Chapter 8

Beneteau's boots thumped the boardwalk as he walked down Devils Lake's busy front street. He paused to read a bulletin board. A man thumbing through wanted posters looked up at him.

"Looks like they're after another half breed who's gone loco," the man said.

"How's that?" Beneteau said, pushing back the brim of his sombrero.

"Says here," the man went on pointing to the top wanted poster hanging on a stack, "a half breed shot and killed an unarmed man in Deadwood, then bushwhacked an old gold miner north of Pleasant Valley. I read about it in the Devil's Chronicle. Weekly paper said a posse has been trailing him and his gang for a couple of weeks."

"Damned breeds," Beneteau said. "Never know what they're up to." He looked at the poster and was relieved that there was no resemblance between himself and the drawing of the desperado. But there was a likeness to Jean Baptiste. Beneteau smiled to himself and crossed the rutted street diagonally.

He headed for French Louis Peltier's hardware store. The bell on the door no more than tinkled as he entered and Beneteau recognized the shapely brunette at the counter before she turned.

"Phillipe Beneteau," Maria said, when he stood beside her.

"Maria," Beneteau said. He grasped her outstretched hand and stooped to brush her cheek with a small kiss.

"What are you doing here?" Beneteau said, heart thumping out of rhythm with his faltering voice.

The Métis woman's dark eyes fell away, then looked back at him and they revealed her interest.

"We're in town trading, getting ready for the hunt, you know. And you, Phillipe Beneteau, what have you been up to?"

Beneteau hadn't felt this good in a month. He almost forgot why he had come to the store.

"We'll talk about it later," he said, finally. The clerk had returned to the counter with a bolt of red cloth for Maria to inspect.

"Is Louis in?" Beneteau asked.

"He's in back in his office," the clerk said.

"Are you camped by the island?" Beneteau said to Maria before slipping through the counter to see the store owner.

"Yes, on the north side of Graham's Island," she said.

"I'll see you there this evening and we'll catch up," he said. "I have some resupplying to do, too."

Beneteau fumbled for an explanation when he tossed the small pouch of gold on French Louis' desk and asked its value?

The full–blooded Frenchman dumped the contents on a small scale.

“I’d say, $30 worth. No questions asked,” said the Frenchman.

“You wouldn’t believe me anyway,” Beneteau said.

“I wouldn’t be in business at all, if everyone who came in here had to explain where he got his money,” French Louis said. “By the way, they are looking for a half breed gang that killed and robbed an old South Dakota gold miner. They watch this place pretty close when there is trouble with breeds,” French Louis said.

“You know they say all kinds of things about us that are not true,” said Beneteau. “French Louis, I need 12 boxes of fourty-four ammunition.”

“Going hunting?” French Louis said.

“Yep, hunting,” Beneteau said.

The clerk interrupted and told the store owner he was wanted at the counter.

Beneteau watched through the thin drapes as French Louis approached the counter to talk to two men. The Frenchman shrugged and threw his hands at arm’s length before turning and heading back to his office. The men left.

“I’ll be right back,” he said to Beneteau. He returned to the store counter and brought back a stack of cartridge boxes with him in a bag and suggested Beneteau use the back door.

“Those men were sheriff’s deputies. They were nosing around about if I had seen any breeds being loose with their spending money. I told them people who buy in my store work hard for their money.” The store owner also laid two stacks of silver dollars totaling $20 on the table.

Beneteau gave French Louis the miner's will to read.

"You could leave this with me," the store owner said. "I could keep it for evidence in a trial, if it ever comes to that."

"That would help," Beneteau said, indifferent to the document's legal importance. He pocketed the $20, thanked the store owner and departed through the back door into the alley with the bag of cartridges. He was half way to the street when a man stepped from a back doorway and pointed at him.

"That's him. That's the son of a bitch who shot and killed my brother," the man said.

Beneteau recognized Cal and his mean, bearded friend, Blackie, but the other man was wearing a badge.

Beneteau slid into the narrow opening between two wooden stores and sprinted back to the front street. He was across the street and into another store before the men behind appeared from the alley.

"Excuse me, miss," Beneteau said to a young woman dressing a mannequin. "Do you have a back door I could use?"

She pointed to the aisle and said to follow it to the rear of the store.

Beneteau moved agilely down the sawdust–covered floor and disappeared through the back door. He was at a full sprint as he ran through a residential yard, then slowed to a fast walk when he cut back to Main Street and melted into the foot traffic of other shoppers.

"Hinhanska, you look worried," said Horace when Beneteau approached where the horses were tethered.

"If we don't get out of here quick, we're going to have hell to pay," Beneteau said, dumping the bag of cartridges in his saddlebags. "Let's get going."

As they rode toward the island, Beneteau told the others of the wanted poster and being spotted and chased by the law.

"So now I, a holy man, am wanted by the law because I ride a mule with a gang of half–breed outlaws," said Horace Throckmorton Bunny III when Beneteau had finished.

"If I had my way, you'd be tucked away safely with your Mandan people on the other side of the big river," Beneteau said.

"You say the wanted poster had a drawing of me on it?" said Jean Baptiste.

"Yep, I suppose they couldn't very well put a drawing of a white man on the poster," Beneteau said. "Lucky you look like just about any other Métis in the country."

Ti Jacques laughed. "You're finally going to make something of yourself, Jean Baptiste. You're going to be famous. It must be your moustache—you handsome outlaw."

"I don't want to be dangling from a cottonwood tree for something I didn't do. Gees, Phillipe, why did you have to take the old man's gold?"

"It wouldn't have made much difference. These white men make up the law as they go along. They'd have accused us of killing him no matter what," Beneteau said.

"I guess, Phillipe, that I wasn't so bad after all when I got drunk and in a fight back at the river crossing," Ti Jacques said. "I wonder what they'll say about us being there."

Beneteau didn't answer, just decided to ride off the main trail leading to the Métis camp.

When they came to Graham's Island, they angled toward it but stayed back from the water until Beneteau spied a half dozen Red River carts at the edge of the lake where camp–fire smoke rose from the brush tops.

"Mr. Bunny. You ride that mule down there and find out if anyone has been to the camp looking for us," Beneteau said. "Tell them who you are and for someone to signal with shots if it's safe for us to come in."

"Mr. Beneteau, am I not part of the wanted gang?" he said. "What if I am captured?"

"If they take you, we'll get you free," Beneteau said. "But if one or all of us got caught, you wouldn't be much good to help us. Just get going?"

Opportunity never held the lead position before and balked at Horace's urging. Beneteau rode up behind the mule and whacked its rear with his hat. The mule bolted, unseating the Medicine Man, who rose from the ground glaring at Beneteau.

Ti Jacques retrieved the mule and Jean Baptiste helped him mount again. "Steady there, Opportunity," he said to the long-eared animal. "And no more biting." While Horace remounted, the mule stepped hard on Jean Baptiste's foot. He dropped his hold on the halter and the mule deftly side stepped, dropping the Medicine Man on the ground again.

"Damned cussed critter," Horace said. "Stand still or I'll blow your brains out." He pushed his Derringer into the animal's ear, which twitched when it heard the hammer cock. "Give me a hand," he said to Ti Jacques, who helped the old man back on. With a kick from each foot in the ribs, robe flowing behind, the mule and Medicine Man set out at a rapid walk to the campground.

"How would we ever get along without them?" Beneteau said. The three Métis men laughed as they watched the odd pair.

A good half hour passed before they heard two well–spaced shots ring out, signaling they were cleared to enter the camp.

The three Métis galloped in and were relieved to be among their own kind. Horace Throckmorton Bunny III was already seated on a log at the side of a campfire.

"Come, Mr. Beneteau," he said as Beneteau dismounted and tied his horse to a cart wheel. "Have some coffee and some of this great tripe." The Medicine Man hacked away at the stomach lining lying on a tin plate and devoured the corn and wild rice it had been stuffed with.

Little children darted back and forth in play among the wagons and their busy mothers. The men rested against the cart wheels, some smoking their pipes, others cleaning rifles. Only one came to see them, although others waved or nodded.

"Henri, good to see you," Beneteau said.

Maria's father Henri Larocque was the boss of this supply train. He took Beneteau's extended hand and shook it gently. "I thought you'd be riding straight to the Turtle Mountains," he said. "I hear the law is chasing you."

Beneteau explained as best he could how one event had led to another until they had all become wanted men.

"More cattle are coming, too," he said. "Lots of them. I saw a bunch and Ti Jacques and Jean Baptiste say they found buffalo only along the west side of the Yellowstone."

Henri said the hunters' numbers were down, too, this year. The Métis were spreading out into Canada to hunt and trap, or even taking up homesteads being opened in the Turtle Mountain area.

"Politics is turning everything upside down. Louis Riel is spoiling for another fight with the Canucks," Henri said.

"I suppose," said Beneteau, "but we will have this hunt, even if it is our last."

"You best keep moving if they are on your trail," said Henri.

"I know," said Beneteau. He joined the others at the campfire.

"Mr. Beneteau, I will be happy to minister among your people," Horace said.

"I suppose you would," Beneteau said. "They are mostly Catholic and have little need of your prattle."

"Prattle is it now? How soon you have forgotten the lessons I've taught you," the Medicine Man said.

"Eat up, boys," Beneteau said. "We've got to head on out to keep these good folks from harm's way."

"Gees, Phillipe," Jean Baptiste said. "I thought we was going to stay comfortable for the rest of the way."

"You big horse," Ti Jacques said. "It'll take this wagon train three days to make the time we can in a day. Phillipe is right."

Phillipe Beneteau saw Maria brushing her horse near a grove of buffalo berry bushes and he went to her.

"Get your shopping done?" he said. "I never thought I'd be seeing you down this far from home."

"I suppose you think men are the only ones who should be allowed out," she replied.

"Some women do pretty much what they want," he said.

"From the sound of it, you have been doing the same," she said.

"You know," he said, "that I was sent out to scout on cattle herds coming here. There's some who figure there will soon be no buffalo left, no room to roam. And it is true. More cattle are pouring into the last buffalo grounds."

"But why is the law after you?" she said.

Beneteau told of the quarrel in Deadwood, avoiding the part of buying the lady a drink. And he explained how he and Horace Throckmorton Bunny III had found the old miner and his will.

"Why don't you go to the sheriff and show him the will?" she asked.

"Because they still want me for shooting a man in Deadwood."

"But that sounds like self defense to me," Maria said.

"I wish you were the judge," Beneteau said. "Anyhow, we'll be moving on. I just wanted to tell you how much." He faltered. "How much I enjoyed seeing you. I suppose you're getting about ready to marry one of your boyfriends."

"As a matter of truth, Phillipe Beneteau, I am. But I don't think he is ready to marry me."

"Who is the lucky cuss?" Beneteau said, his heart sinking.

"You'll just have to keep your eyes open to find out," she told him. She untied her horse, a rangy sorrel, and led him away for water.

Phillipe Beneteau, head a little giddy from watching her walk, returned to his gang of outlaws.

"Opportunity is dying to move on, Hinhanska," said Horace.

"Sure hope you can keep up, Mr. Bunny," said Jean Baptiste. "From here on, there gets to be more and more white people and they don't trust nobody, especially full–blooded Indians."

"But we'll take care of you," said Ti Jacques.

"Hmmmmph," said Horace. "You seem to be in a good bit of trouble yourselves without even trying. Let's go, Opportunity," he said.

Phillipe Beneteau trotted the piebald at the head of their little troop and they cut back away from the river, pausing on a hill to wave back at camp onlookers, among whom Beneteau saw Maria mounted and watching from the riverbank.

They were all saddle weary when lantern lights popped out of the Turtles at dusk the following day.

The village had quieted for the evening but still one could hear a pump handle creaking at a well, or an ax splitting wood. Someone played a lively fiddle tune in one yard they rode past. Dancers were too busy jigging to even notice them pass.

Beneteau liked the feeling of familiarity. It had been a long, eventful trip. Disappointing, too. He had confirmed that more cattle were being trailed further north. From the south it was cattle. From the north, it was Canadian settlers with the Métis in the middle.

They turned their horses out to pasture and Ti Jacques and Jean Baptiste went to their log homes. Phillipe Beneteau took Horace Throckmorton Bunny III with him to Koohkoum Emma's.

The dark-skinned woman at the flat–topped cook stove looked up when Beneteau entered right behind his familiar knock.

"Phillipe," she cried and ran to him and threw her arms around him.

"Grandma, like you to meet our preacher friend Mr. Bunny. He is a Mandan I picked up north of Deadwood and he's been hanging in ever since."

"You poor man," she said to Horace. "Most of the Métis men don't like to be with Phillipe because he acts like a white man most of the time."

"Ma'am, he has been little problem for me, but I have burdened him with my effort to give spiritual knowledge."

"Spiritual doesn't sound anything like Phillipe Beneteau to me," she said. "I suppose you men are starving. Sit a spell and I'll fetch something to eat."

They were finishing their first cup of coffee when a plate of venison steaks arrived.

"For a spiritual man, you sure have a good appetite," Beneteau told Horace.

"One thing I learned among white people was that one never loses the taste of food from his past. I cut my teeth on venison," said Horace.

"Cut most of 'em right out, too," Beneteau said. He smiled but kept his eyes averted from the Medicine Man's, so he didn't see him glare.

"One should never call attention to another's faults in polite company," Horace said.

"Aw, you're among family now, Mr. Bunny. Relax."

"What religion does Mr. Bunny profess?" said Koohkoum Emma.

"I am an ordained Baptist minister," said Horace,"but I still adhere to my Mandan beliefs. You'd be surprised at the similarities between my people's Lone Man and Jesus."

"I tried to tell him that most of our people are Catholic, but it hasn't slowed him down a bit," said Beneteau.

"Be civil now, Phillipe," she said.

"That has become my most recent cross to bear," said Horace. "Trying to make Mr. Beneteau a little civil."

"Well, you two just go ahead and talk religion," Beneteau said. "I'm going outside for some fresh air and a smoke."

The night air brushed his face as Phillipe Beneteau loaded his grandma's corn cob pipe with a pinch of tobacco. The village had grown quiet. Beneteau wandered down to the corral where Opportunity and Bronc stood grazing in the moonlight. Beneteau whistled through his teeth and the piebald's ears perked before he trotted over. Beneteau was waiting with a bucket of oats he had scooped from a grain shed at the side of the flat–roofed pole barn.

The horse nickered before stretching its neck to reach the oats. "You're a good boy for getting me home," Beneteau said patting the big horse's neck. "But we kind of miss old Buster, don't we?" Opportunity stood off aloof to the camaraderie between the man and his horse.

Beneteau turned and headed for the bunk bed he knew grandma had prepared for him and Horace Throckmorton Bunny III.

"Hinhanska," the old Medicine Man said when Beneteau came through the door. "I like your people." His bony legs hung from the edge of the bed to his gnarled feet which rested flat against the rough pine floor.

"Wait until they march you off to church tomorrow morning," Beneteau said, recalling the next day ahead of them was Sunday.

"When one has been ordained to do the Lord's work, one does not mind going to church," said Horace.

Beneteau reached in his saddle bag and brought out the sack in which he had left half the cartridges. He rummaged in it until he found a knotted kerchief which he untied. He withdrew a silver dollar which he tossed to the Medicine Man. "If you want to make a good impression, tomorrow, Mr. Bunny, toss this in the collection basket when it is passed around."

"The Lord does truly provide," said Horace Throckmorton Bunny III. "My Mandan people collect too, just food and clothing, not money," he said. "And the Baptists taught me that you can't run a church on hot air. They also collect money. Strange how we have different religions but similar practices."

"You're getting a little too deep for me, Mr. Bunny," Beneteau said, blowing out the lantern. "I need some sleep." Beneteau could hear the Medicine Man's voice drone on in the dark. His own thoughts turned to recalling how easily he could recognize Maria from behind with just a glance at her hair and tight wool riding pants.

Then it was morning and the moment Beneteau stepped out of the bunkhouse he could smell bacon and eggs coming from grandma's kitchen.

"Be going to church today, Phillipe?" she asked when he came in to get a towel to dry his face after giving it a dunking from the basin by the well.

"You know me, Koohkoum Emma," he said. "Just funerals and my own wedding, if that's what it takes to get the woman I want for a wife."

"You still eying Maria Larocque?" she said.

"You'll just have to wait and see," he said.

"Phillipe, I do wish you'd take a wife and settle down. You won't be young and handsome forever."

"Pass the bacon and eggs, please, Koohkoum," he said.

"I feel great this morning," said the Medicine Man when he came in.

"Are you going to wear that getup to church this morning?" Beneteau said. The Medicine Man looked as if he had just stuck his head through a tattered canvas tent.

"You have not read the Bible on John the Baptist," the Medicine Man said. "You came upon me in the wilderness, Mr. Beneteau."

"And you were wearing the same clothes then as now," Beneteau said.

"And I am the same person now as then," said Horace. "Unfortunately, so are you, Mr. Beneteau."

"You boys better have some coffee," said Koohkoum Emma. "And don't you worry about how you're dressed. You look fine to me, Mr. Bunny."

Phillipe Beneteau saddled Bronc after breakfast and headed out to check the horses and few head of cattle the Métis had grazing in the surrounding hills. It wasn't long and he was joined by Ti Jacques, who also used checking on the livestock as an excuse to escape going to church. The two men exchanged greetings, then dismounted to sit on the bare ground for a smoke.

"We weren't the only ones having trouble," said Ti Jacques through a puff of blue smoke he blew out in the clear morning air.

"How's that?" Beneteau said, irritated that Ti Jacques interrupted his thoughts about how nice a morning it was. Meadow larks warbled nearby as he watched a muskrat swim across a small pool of water that had built behind an old beaver dam.

"A bunch of Canadian Métis visited a week ago trying to get our people to fight with them against Canadian settlers taking their land on the Red River."

"I suppose land grabbers are stirring them up," Beneteau said. It seemed to him that no one could see the change that was taking place in the Métis lifestyle; except for a handful of old men, no one believed. Land space shrunk even more after more forced cessions to the U.S. government in 1882. The Turtle Mountains were unable to handle the amount of

Chippewa and Métis. Chief Little Shell had petitioned the U.S. government for more land for his people. There was talk that there might be some allotments west along the Yellowstone River.

"Ti Jacques," he said to his friend. "Have you ever thought about raising cattle and horses for a living?"

"You mean like a white man?" Ti Jacques said.

"Nope, like a Métis," Beneteau said.

"You've got about as much chance of that as becoming the Great White Father in Washington," Ti Jacques said.

"You mean because we're breeds?" said Beneteau.

"We all know you think you are a white man," said Ti Jacques. "But inside you are just like me, Phillipe—born to chase the buffalo and hunt wild geese and deer and to trap in winter.

I don't know," Beneteau said. "I just think about it and wish you would, too. You can't stop things changing, but you can learn to roll with it like a tumbleweed in a strong wind. Those weeds find a place to rest and grow again."

"You know me and Jean Baptiste will ride with you. But we only know how to ride and hunt. That's our life. We can fight for that."

Phillipe Beneteau knew he would be called on after church to report what he had learned while he was away. And then, he hoped that Maria Larocque would arrive by afternoon. He really wanted to talk to her before she hooked up with some rival.

Chapter 9

It was mid morning when Beneteau and Ti Jacques entered the round log structure that was the village meeting place. They spied Jean Baptiste and joined him.

Other men walked in to take up space along the walls. Some sat on benches, others plopped down on the floor. Four men flanked Henri Larocque, who stood in the room's center.

Henri opened the meeting by asking Father Belgarde to bless them. The priest stepped forward from the edge of the building and while they bowed their heads he called on the Creator for guidance in this undertaking.

"Let's get right to it," Henri said when he had their attention again. "Are you Métis ready to hunt?"

The men broke into applause, some hooting war cries, which drew laughter.

Henri gave a tally on how many carts would be making the trip. Only about 50 this year. Cousins to the north from Pembina and Canada along the Red River had not come down. They were tied up with Louis Riel, he said. "Some of our people have left to join him," he said. "But we are Americans as well as Métis. This big land is our home, not France, not Canada. "We have had scouts out looking for the buffalo and keeping an eye on what the white men are up to. There is change in the wind and we will adapt to it just as we have to being both red and white, but first we will hunt the buffalo as we have always done."

After the boot stomping, hooting and applause settled down, Henri called for scouting reports.

"Mr. D'or Métis," he said to Beneteau, "what did you learn among your people the white men?" Beneteau's eyes did not betray the rancor he felt from the remark. Golden Métis he was called for he was of a lighter skin, but Phillipe Antoine Beneteau also knew who he really was.

"Brothers," he said. "Most of you know that I was sent out to scout rumors of more cattle being driven into the hunting grounds we share with the full bloods."

"There's no secret that our brother buffalo are getting thinned by hunters and being crowded out of their native range."

"I have seen thousands of more cattle being driven north to Dakota Territory."

"Our elders have told us that the days of the hunt will come to an end. It will be harder on the full bloods. Most never learned much about white farming methods or raising cattle. They won't even build a cart."

"But Métis can change if we want to. In my heart, I am sad to say this. This may be the last time we chase our big friends as we have done in the old days. You should remember this hunt like no one before for it may be your last."

There was only perfunctory applause. Phillipe Beneteau had not told them what they wanted to hear.

Jean Baptiste was greeted warmly when he rose to speak. He said that he and Ti Jacques had scouted from Turtle Mountains to the Yellowstone River.

“The biggest herd we found was west of the river. There was a few thousand head. It’s not just cattle driving out the buffalo. They’re being killed for sport by white hunters,” he said.

Henri Larocque took over the meeting again and described the order of the hunt and appointed captains for five groups.

“Is everybody ready?” he asked them.

They stomped their boots, hooted and cried their assent.

“We leave in the morning then,” Henri said. “Meeting adjourned.”

Beneteau left to put his belongings in order and to split the ammunition he purchased with his two friends, who followed him to Koohkoum Emma’s.

“Hinhanska,” said Horace Throckmorton Bunny III when they came into her log house. “I’ve been learning a lot about you. Koohkoum says you never were good about going to church. You see, my purpose becomes more clear.”

“Mr. Bunny, it would be nice if you would stay here with her while we hunt,” Beneteau said.

“Ah, but you will need all the spiritual help you can get,” said Horace.

“We’ve always done well without you in the past. We have Father Belgarde for our spiritual leader.”

“Mr. Beneteau,” said the Medicine Man. “When Koohkoum’s Chippewa ancestors and my Mandans and all the red men from the plains and mountains hunted buffalo, there were buffalo from here to Mexico. We thought the Creator’s bounty would never end. But then the white man came from the

Creator's bounty. And we thought that must be good, too. We thought they were gods sent down among us. But we found out too late that the white gods weren't gods, nor were they wise. I learned that it was true they did not follow the words of the Savior. It is better to give than to receive and you must love your brother. The spiritual leaders didn't teach the word that was given them. And so their error has spread and the buffalo are almost gone. You, Hinhanska, have the blood of both the white man and red in your veins. I am here to see to it that you listen to your red ancestors. Father Belgarde can govern your debt to your white people."

"I guess that means you are coming with us," Beneteau said.

"And I am, too, Phillipe," said Koohkoum Emma. "Who will boil the bones and make the bundles of pemmican? You must have a woman on the trail."

"Koohkoum is right," said Jean Baptiste. "You're no hand at lady's work, Phillipe."

Beneteau split the bullets three ways. He asked Horace to help Koohkoum sharpen the skinning knives while he went to make a final check of their cart and oxen. God, he couldn't stand those plodding beasts, but they were the backbone of the hunt.

"Good morning, Phillipe Beneteau," Maria said, looking up from filing her horse's front hooves.

"Is your family ready?" Beneteau said, knowing that Henri Larocque was always ready. His daughter had not come by her horse knowledge entirely on her own.

"Yes," she said. "Is there anything I can do for you?" Maria also knew that Phillipe Beneteau's family was only his grand-mother and she was getting old.

Beneteau was already mesmerized by just the sound of her voice. She had blossomed into a full–breasted young woman whose backside was firm from riding. Her glistening jet black hair was knotted in a pony tail tied with a crimson ribbon. Her grey wool pants were tucked in knee–length, beaded moccasins and her paisley cotton shirt was gathered at the waist by a traditional Métis sash. He was unglued by her presence.

"Maria," he said, unable to sort through his emotions. "Why, good morning. I didn't expect to bump into you so soon."

"I thought you wanted to know if we are ready for the hunt," she said.

"That's right," he said. "I also wanted you to know it is a good morning."

"I think it is a nice morning," she said. "Would you hold Chief while I finish this hoof?"

He looked down on the roundness of her breasts where her shirt broke at the collar as she kneeled before him. The horse nuzzled his hand holding the halter rope.

"Where's your fancy six gun, Phillipe?" she said without looking up. "I always loved that gun."

"I lost it," he said.

"You must have lost Buster, too." Koohkoum had told her the story the old woman had gleaned from Horace Throckmorton Bunny III.

Beneteau reached to the ground and picked up the tongs beside Maria.

"If you ever get finished there, I'll trim his back hoofs."

"Oh sure, big strong man. I'll take care of Chief's hooves. You just hold onto him."

"I kinda liked that little raccoon," he said.

"I thought you were going to marry him," she said. "But he sure was a sweet little guy. I use to feed him berries right out of my hand."

"He was okay," Beneteau said. He looked out toward the sun on the horizon and its rays highlighted the anger and sadness in his eyes.

"Why did you bring Mr. Bunny here?" she said.

"Couldn't get rid of him," Beneteau said after clearing his throat. "Damnedest person I've ever been around. Always got something to say. Other than cookin' and spouting off, he don't do much else of anything."

She paused, then rummaged in a rawhide bag that held her few tools. She extracted an oilskin package and held it out to Beneteau. "Here," she said "take this. It was my grandfather's. Papa says a hunter should always have one of these to finish a bad job."

Beneteau's hand sagged under the weight of the package when she thrust it toward him.

Unwrapped, the package revealed a worn but well kept ball and cap Army Colt.

"I'm sorry, Maria, but I can't accept this," he said.

"You must," she said. "I already have my own handgun. We'd hate to have you gored by a wounded buffalo. There are too few of us left."

"Then my first buffalo will be dedicated to the Larocques," he said.

"Dedicate it to my grandfather and Koohkoum Emma."

When they were finished with Chief, they strode silently side by side back to the center of the village.

"See you in the morning," she said.

Beneteau watched her continue up the road to the Larocque place. He thought back to the day at the swimming hole and reminded himself that some good things just get better with age. But who was she interested in? He hoped she hadn't picked her man yet.

He went to the barn and inspected the cart they would be driving. Koohkoum had already loaded much of their supplies. A cast iron pot for rendering lard. The knives for skinning. Bedding. A canvas tarp for shelter. Some Métis would even bring tipis. She was loading a small supply of kindling in the corner of the cart when he walked up.

"This old cart has been on a few hunts and been repaired many times by grandpa," she said.

"I hope it holds up for this one," he said, wobbling one of the five–foot high wheels. It seemed sound. The wagon box was topped by oak arches for fastening the tarp for a roof.

Beneteau was glad he was an outrider. He had never grown accustomed to the high–pitched wailing of their wagon wheels which ascended to the heavens and stretched to the horizon when the caravan was on the march.

"Oh, Phillipe," she said, "I am so happy to get to go on this hunt. A woman loves to see new country and the flowers are so beautiful in the spring. Your grandfather was a great hunter."

Beneteau had grown up listening to the stories of hunts gone by. He had even learned the old method of holding musket balls in his mouth to load his gun while chasing a buffalo.

After firing the first shot, a Métis hunter poured a charge of powder down the barrel, spit in a new ball and slammed the butt against his boot to settle the charge. All while continuing the chase at a full gallop. A repeating rifle like his Henry gave the hunter a new edge in a dangerous game.

He had heard of men being thrown from their horses and stomped or gored to death. Without a priest along to settle their differences, men had gunned each other down over claiming rights to a kill. Nothing he ever heard had frightened him.

Women like Maria looked favorably on good hunters and the hides and pemmican brought in income the womenfolk also liked. Money gave men power to buy new horses, new guns. Those who made the trek to St. Paul got to see sights of another world and came back full of great stories. And they brought back bolts of cloth, pots and beads so the Métis could continue their trade with full bloods.

It was sad to think that this lifestyle was ending, but Phillipe Beneteau rationalized that it was also so when the Métis had to give up a woodland life of hunting and trapping to become plainsmen of commerce.

"Even a rabbit changes the color of its coat for the season," his grandpa used to say.

Finally, satisfied that their gear was all properly stowed and ready for the march, Beneteau saddled Bronc for a ride in the hills.

He was musing by a pond formed from a beaver dam when the brush crashed and Ti Jacques and Jean Baptiste broke through on horseback.

"The sheriff just paid us a visit," Jean Baptiste said without a greeting.

"Said he was looking for you, Phillipe. Said, French Louis had tipped him that you admitted to killing that old miner when you sold him the gold. Gees, Phillipe, I thought you said you gave French Louis the will to prove your innocence."

"I did," Beneteau said. "That son of a bitch."

"We told him you went on to Canada," Ti Jacques said. "Don't know if he bought it, he'll probably keep an eye on our hunting party for a spell."

"Can one of you drive our cart? I'll join up with you after two days," Beneteau said.

"Koohkoum said not to worry. She and Mr. Bunny will do just fine," Jean Baptiste said. "Here, Phillipe, she made you something to eat and we put a box of fourty-four's in there." He handed Beneteau the bedroll that contained his supplies.

Beneteau didn't waste time. He got on Bronc and they disappeared into the the brush without looking back. They glided along an old game trail that led toward the western edge of the Turtles. Beneteau thought hard about why French Louis would double cross him but he couldn't come up with a reason. The Frenchman had always been a little crooked but no one had ever accused him of being a spy for the law. There was a small reward being offered, but French Louis didn't need the money. Beneteau decided he better concentrate on getting out of range of the sheriff's jurisdiction. The sheriff, too, was familiar with the Turtle Mountains.

The piebald's ears perked and his flared eyes stared at a bend coming up on the trail. Beneteau, sensing the horse's tension in his own legs, stepped lithely to the ground, unsheathed the Henry and led the horse forward with the reins. Bronc reared and pulled back at the same instant a mother black bear came charging up the trail. The Henry popped out of his hand before he could sight it on the bear. As the animal closed on him, Beneteau's fingers closed on the old Colt's steel body. The hammer cocked in its swing up and without aiming, Beneteau fired the first shot at the bear's lowered head. He continued to crank off round after round until the black bear crumpled almost at his feet. Bronc stood quivering but 10 yards away. Beneteau nudged the bear's head with his boot while he reloaded. Blood oozed from the animal's forehead and shoulders where shots had penetrated.

"We haven't got time to skin this critter and take its meat, Bronc," he said more to himself than the horse.

Bronc still was edgy when Beneteau mounted him and they

continued on the trail. Twin bear cubs romped into sight and followed them. The horse wouldn't settle down, so Beneteau put him to a canter and they quickly outdistanced the cubs.

"Damn," was all Beneteau could manage. The cub's mother was dead, his horse was spooked, he had left good meat to rot and he had been forced to give away his position by gunfire. And he was being chased for a crime he never committed. Beneteau even let it cross his mind that maybe he should go to church once in awhile. Ah, not for a spell. Maria could get him into a church. But he found his God in the natural setting. And right now in the darkness of the woods, he was comfortable despite his woes.

"Good boy," he said to Bronc. He patted the horse's neck affectionately. Worrying about the commotion that came from killing the bear, Beneteau decided to circle and check his back trail. Fox, coyote and deer did it all the time. They headed toward a small rock cliff from which gurgled a spring that created a path through the woods as its stream tumbled downward to a valley. Beneteau tied Bronc to a tree and crept forward to the edge of the trees where his view was unobstructed to the game trail he had passed over earlier.

Muffled voices reached his ears. He watched three men ride into view below him. He recognized the man called Cal, his black–bearded companion and the sheriff. Anger rose in his chest at the sight of the mean one. He would have stalked the outsiders if Sheriff Hansen wasn't with them. He would have loved to have ended this chase up in these mountains he knew so well. But the sheriff was only doing his duty, or what he thought was his duty. The other two men were blinded by their hatred and deserved to die. Beneteau watched them disappear and figured he must now ride north to divert them. He would lose them in the north country and catch up with the wagon train as best he could.

The wagons were circled, their shafts jetting skyward like a giant centipede on its back when Beneteau sat on Bronc eying their fires from a hillock. A lively fiddle blessed the exit of the sun which was edging from view in a mixture of pink and orange splashed through a backdrop of grey turning black. It had taken him three days to catch up with the train. The guards had dug rifle pits around the perimeter of the camp. A horse herd and oxen milled on nearby grass. A section of the wagon circle was open into which the animals could be driven if the train was attacked.

Beneteau fired a two-shot salute, which was answered by two more for all clear. He put Bronc into a trot and sat erect as they moved toward the prairie fort. He exchanged nods with the guard he passed, then closed on the opening for livestock where he dismounted and tied Bronc to a wagon wheel before continuing on foot.

A small sea of faces surrounding the central camp seemed to dance in the reflection of the flames. The fiddle player's silhouette bobbed and weaved to his music. Hardly anyone noticed Beneteau but his eyes had already picked out Maria seated near her father in the front row of spectators.

Beneteau went in search of Koohkoum Emma and her escort Horace Throckmorton Bunny III.

"Ah, Hinhanska," said Horace, "we were just speaking about you," the old man said when Beneteau found them.

"We were beginning to worry," said Koohkoum Emma." Did you have any problems, grandson?" She rose and went to a pot hanging over her own small campfire. "Come, get a bowl of this stew. Mr. Bunny says it is the most delicious food he has had ever."

Beneteau grabbed a tin soup bowl and a wooden spoon from a stack piled on a weathered cutting board Koohkoum Emma used for her kitchen. But before he could get to the fire, he remembered Bronc.

"Nope, no problems," he answered. "I better put Bronc away. Save some of that food for me, though. Mr. Bunny, I hope you have taken good care of my grandmother."

"You just tend to your horse," the old man said. "We've been getting along just fine."

Beneteau left to attend to his horse, which was gone when he got back to the camp entryway. He heard a light whistle in the dark, then a woman's voice.

"I've got Bronc over here for water and oats," Maria said to him. "I figured you must be tired, Phillipe, getting in so late. I saw you when you came in."

Beneteau made out their dark shadows. The familiar smell of his horse mingled with some flowery odor coming from Maria. He thought she was sweet enough without wearing that buck lure.

His hand touched hers when he took the lead rope attached to Bronc's halter.

"I was beginning to worry about you," she said softly.

Instinctively, he slid his hand along her arm to the firmness of her small waist.

"I kinda missed you, too," he said awkwardly before he bent to her face. When she didn't move he brought his lips to hers and she pulled him gently to her where he felt the softness of her breasts against his chest.

"Maria," the voice of Henri Larocque yelled from the camp entry. "Are you out there, dear?

She pulled back from Beneteau and yelled back, "I'm at the water hole, helping Phillipe Beneteau put his horse away."

"Well, you better get on in here and hit the sack. We'll be rising early in the morning."

"Okay, papa," she said, giving Beneteau's hand a little squeeze before she left him.

He pegged Bronc in the darkness now being lit by hundreds of fireflies, then he returned to his own camp. He had just gone from being a man who didn't think he had any reason to live except survival to one who had a whole new world before him. Whoever Maria had an eye on, she had not ruled him entirely out of the running. And he knew in his heart already that he had never in such a short encounter felt this way about a woman before.

"That was quick, Phillipe," Koohkoum Emma said when he returned.

"Come, Hinhanska, enjoy the night air and tell us what you've been doing the past three days," said Horace.

Beneteau filled his plate with stew and Koohkoum poured him a cup of coffee. Beneteau sat on the ground and used a cart wheel for a backrest.

Koohkoum clanked around the fire putting her pots and pans in order while washing tin plates and cups left from the evening meal.

"It appears to me," said Horace when Beneteau failed to respond, "that I am now more important to you then ever. Not only am I your Indian spiritual advisor, but now your legal advisor, too. You should never have left that will with the Frenchman. Your kinsmen can't read. Not even you, White Owl, can read. But I can read and I read the old miner's will. You should learn to treat me with respect, my grandson," Horace said, his eyes twinkling in the firelight as he watched Koohkoum Emma in her outdoor kitchen.

Beneteau arose and strode to the fire where he dumped his plate in the wash water, then poured himself another cup of coffee.

"Mr. Bunny been behaving?" he said to Koohkoum Emma.

"Oh, we're getting along fine," she said.

"You are a clever man, Mr. Bunny," Beneteau said when he plopped back on the ground by Horace Throckmorton Bunny III. "I sure hope you don't start lying and cheating like everybody else."

"My people are not liars," Horace said. "We have always been willing to make a deal between white men or red men, although some like the cutthroat Sioux have been hard to get along with."

"I hope you aren't planning to make a deal with me," said Beneteau. He watched Koohkoum settle down on a small wooden milking stool she used for a chair. Head bowed, the old woman mended a pair of moccasins. She looked up between stitches and watched the two men, then went back to her sewing.

"I plan no deal with you, White Owl. Spiritual advisors need no deals with mortal men. We have made our commitment to the Creator. But we have worldly needs, too."

"Look, Mr. Bunny, if you've got ideas about settling in with my grandmother, forget it. She is getting along fine."

"You younger people just don't understand your elders' needs for companionship," said Horace.

"I'll let Koohkoum be my guide," Beneteau said.

"I am your guide, my grandson. We have already decided to become one."

Beneteau shook his head, breathed deeply, then shook his head again. "I'll be damned," he said. "Now you're going to be my grandfather, too."

Beneteau looked up at the sound of footsteps approaching.

"Phillipe Beneteau," Henri Larocque said when he stepped into the circle of light. "I want you to take the night watch on the west outpost." The outpost was the rifle pit dug farthest away from the camp.

"Anything you say, Henri," Beneteau replied. "Are you expecting trouble?"

"You never know," said Henri. "Keep a sharp watch." The camp leader continued on his rounds.

Beneteau wondered if Henri picked him for his skill, or just to get him out of camp and away from Maria. He got his Henry and bedroll and said good night to Koohkoum and Horace.

Chapter 10

Beneteau crept catlike in the dark toward the dark form sitting in front of him. When he was within five yards, he tossed a small rock toward the depression of the rifle pit he knew was there. The guard flinched and Beneteau rose to his haunches and lunged onto the surprised guard's back.

"Gotcha!" he said.

"Phillipe Beneteau, you crazy son of a bitch," the man said. "I almost killed you."

Beneteau ran the cold, flat side of his knife blade past the man's neck. "Yeh, I know. I almost feel dead right now. You better get back to camp and get some sleep. I'll take over."

The sentry said no more and turned over his post to Beneteau. He knew he had been caught off guard. That the man was napping alerted Beneteau to the need to circle his rifle pit in the dark to assure himself that nothing was amiss. Then, Beneteau settled into the boredom he faced before dawn.

A pack of coyotes yipped their pleasure in the night air. The sky hung overhead like a black sea full of sparkling diamonds. Beneteau rolled into the freshly dug rifle pit and propped his

Henry at an angle. He drew the old Army Colt, cocked it half way and spun its cylinder, then holstered it again. He was about as ready as one could get for the nothing he expected to happen.

Then he heard a voice, a raspy whisper.

"Phillipe Beneteau, I brought you a blanket," the voice said.

It was Maria Larocque.

"You snuck up on me," he said when she approached. The Henry was already in his hands at the first sound he heard and the rifle's hammer was cocked as she spoke.

"Can I come?" she said.

"Sure," he replied. "But you better hang onto that blanket. I wouldn't want to get in the habit of having a wrap to keep me warm and I sure wouldn't want any of the men to see me tucked in. Your dad say it was all right for you to be out this late?"

"No," she said, dropping in beside him. "I've just never been allowed on guard duty. So I wanted to see how it is."

Their voices were barely audible when Beneteau cupped his hand over her mouth, then listened. "Sorry, but I've got a job to do," he said.

Maria remained quiet while he peered into the blackness and listened.

"Did you hear something?" she said.

Beneteau didn't answer. It was a far off hissing sound. He pointed his nose skyward like a coyote but sniffed instead of howled.

"Maria, do you smell smoke?" he said. Before she could answer he could see a pulsating orange light on some clouds drifting in from the west. Just one week on the trail and the hunting party had its first test. “We’ve got to alert the wagons there’s a prairie fire coming.”

Maria sprinted back to the circled encampment. By the time she arrived, the camp was astir and her father was issuing orders to wake all families to break camp. Other Métis had good ears and noses. The race now pitted their oxen against the speed of the fire.

Beneteau, who was right behind Maria’s sprinting form, headed to Koohkoum Emma and Horace Throckmorton Bunny III and helped them yoke the ox. He had Bronc saddled when Jean Baptiste showed with orders for them from Henri Larocque to scout out the fire and try to determine if it was man caused or natural.

As they mounted, Ti Jacques galloped up and the three Métis charged off into the dark toward the illuminated horizon. The carts set off a terrifying screeching in the night. Beneteau sensed the determination of the people and their resolve encouraged him and his two companions. The fire was not as distant as it first appeared and it seemed to be widening at an unnatural rate.

“Ride back and tell Henri that we have a bigger problem than nature on our hands,” he said. “I’d say it was the Sioux that set this fire. We’ll go on closer for a look.”

Ti Jacques peeled away in the dark and headed back, the pounding of his horses’s hooves telling the other two Métis that he was sprinting his horse despite the dangers.

“I hope he lets him have his head,” Jean Baptiste said to Beneteau as they listened to the echoing hoof beats fade.

“He will,” Beneteau said. “Jean Baptiste, you cover the north and I’ll take the south. We’ll meet back in the center, but don’t wait for me. Henri needs our reports. And be careful. You know the Sioux will be expecting us.”

The early morning wind had not yet whipped up, so the fire was just crawling forward. Still, Beneteau hung back a quarter of a mile until he arrived at the southern point. He saw the silhouettes of two riders dragging flaming bundles through the grass and he pointed Bronc at them, the Henry now cradled across the saddle. From the corner of his eye, he saw the war party perched across the brow of a small hillock. The warriors charged, yipping their war cries like a pack of coyotes.

Beneteau pulled Bronc to his haunches, fired at the charging warriors and whirled the piebald in the opposite direction by releasing the pressure of his left leg and applying it with his right. The horse was off at full speed again. The sky was beginning to lighten and Beneteau saw Jean Baptiste heading diagonally toward him pursued by another band of Indians. They met in a parallel path and reined their horses back toward the wagon train.

"We'll get some distance between us, then try to stall them," Beneteau shouted. "Use the rifle pits."

The carts were still in sight when they topped the hills that rose above the night camp site. Beneteau and Jean Baptiste raced across the 200 yards of level ground to the perimeter of rifle pits. They leapt from their horses, gave them free rein to continue and dove for cover in the same pit.

Their rifles barked as the charging Sioux came into range and drove past them. Four empty horses continued the charge, their riders unseated by the fusillade of bullets they ran into. One band of Indians split off in pursuit of the Métis horses, the remainder turned and charged again.

Beneteau could see the wagons forming up in a circle in the distance. And a party of 10 Métis quirted their horses to charge out at the Sioux. As Bronc and Jean Baptiste's horse blasted into their midst the Métis grabbed the horses' reins and turned them, then continued their charge.

The warriors reeled under the heavy fire from the Métis repeating rifles, then they spun to take up the fight with Beneteau and Jean Baptiste. Both men were keeping up a rapid fire from the rifle pit. The Indians, though outnumbering their enemies, regrouped and withdrew under the withering fire. Then, they headed toward the wagon train.

Beneteau and Jean Baptiste leapt into their saddles when their mounts were handed back to them and they joined in the race against the Indians back to the carts.

Grey smoke billowed into the sky behind the charging Métis as the wind whipped the prairie fire into a roaring blaze headed toward the circled carts.

The Sioux attack broke off and the warriors disappeared over the horizon, leaving the Métis to defend now against the oncoming prairie fire.

Henri Larocque shouted for the wagon members to keep calm and stay together. Beneteau saw Father Belgarde bent over in prayer.

"What's your plan, Henri," he said from Bronc's back. "That fire's moving right along now with the wind."

"See if you can find us any cover out there," Henri said, pointing to the south and east. "Take two others with you."

Without waiting for more, Beneteau put Bronc to a gallop and was joined as he left the train by Jean Baptiste and Ti Jacques.

Within a half a mile, they found a small round prairie swamp. Jean Baptiste and Ti Jacques were sent back to report their find while Beneteau rode up on the hillsides and circled the area to look for more trouble from the Sioux. He saw the attacking band riding away to avoid the fire they had set.

The fire front billowed thick smoke, which turned into a throat-burning haze as it was swept along by the wind.

Beneteau watched the carts squeal toward him. It looked like it would be close. He took his rawhide lariat and packed its noose with dry grass and tumble weeds, then struck a match to it. He spurred Bronc and they drew the fire pack across the face of the swamp. The dry grass blazed and spread, racing at and around the swamp, leaving behind a blackened swath. The burned out area would afford the Métis carts more protection. The first of the carts moved down the last stretch of open ground.

Beneteau hung his holster and cartridge belt on Bronc's saddle and gave the reins to a young lad who strode afoot by the first wagon that arrived. He grabbed the halter of the ox pulling the cart and led it into the swamp. The depth of the mud increased, but the ox was only in to its belly, when Beneteau slipped into a drop off. He hung there up to his chest, wiggling to regain his footing. That was as far as the wagons could come. The ox held and Beneteau got his feet back under him and turned the beast so the cart could be led in a circle. He shouted to a man to stand at the point of the drop off and keep others from falling in.

"Split some of the wagons right," Beneteau yelled to the man.

Another Métis had the ox towing the second cart hard by his halter and with a stick poked him to a right turn. The fire was bearing down on the rear of the train. Henri Larocque rode up and ordered the carts to make a second line moving left and right. The oxen and carts were lumbered into two lanes of traffic on each side and formed a set of two circles around the swamp. Men, women and children pulled and pushed the carts. Last in line were the riders, who struggled to keep their horses from bolting as sparks flew in the dense smoke headed at them.

"Wet some sacks," shouted Henri Larocque. Métis women dunked any cloth they could find in the swamp, which now oozed a sulfurous smelling water in a trail where the carts had parted the slime. They passed out the wet rags to whoever wanted them. Men hitched the cloth over their horses noses and tied them on their faces. The Métis took on a ghoulish appearance as they eyed the fire driving toward them. Their carts, though, were neatly circled in the swamp and the men held their horses in yet another thin circle. Extra horses and livestock had been left to fend for themselves and would have to be rounded up later.

"That was close," Beneteau said, sidling up to Henri Larocque.

"I think we can thank God and Father Belgarde for our good fortune," Henri said. The priest, mud spattered from head to foot, walked among the people blessing them. A Rosary hung from his hands.

Beneteau figured he had just witnessed Father Belgarde's grace from heaven first hand. Instead of panic, the hunting party had acted with discipline and they were all lucky the swamp showed up.

Henri went off counting noses and organizing an exit from the swamp. The Métis would now have to find a new camp and round up their livestock and horses. The fire roared on its destructive path to the southwest.

"Are you men up to gathering the stock?" he shouted at Beneteau as he rode past on his grey buffalo runner. "Take 10 men, but watch out for those Sioux. We'll move to the west until we find grass and water."

Beneteau first sought out Koohkoum Emma and Horace.

"Hinhanska," the old man said without removing his soggy mask. "What on earth are you people doing? Why don't you make peace with those Indians?" He was perched on the wagon seat and Koohkoum was peering from inside the wagon cover.

"Mr. Bunny. We are at peace with the Sioux. That's their normal way of greeting us. The Sioux figure if everybody is taking their buffalo, they have a right to take whatever they can get in return."

"You Métis didn't give them much," the old man said.

"You'd think they know that by now, but they keep trying. How are you folks?"

"I think we're going to be fine if we can get this contraption back on dry ground," Horace said.

"If you need help, just let someone know," Beneteau said. "We've got to head out to find our animals."

Henri was already leading the last wagons to enter the swamp back onto the blackened prairie. The wagons were radiating straight out where they had come to rest and lumbering forward far enough to make room for the second circle.

Beneteau with seven other men picked by Ti Jacques and Jean Baptiste rode away to find the animals somewhere ahead of the fire.

The first evidence of their escape route was the charred remains of a colt that couldn't keep up with its mother. Then, the smoldering remains of a horse whose left leg appeared shattered at the knee, a victim of a badger burrow into which the horse must have plunged a leg.

Puffs of black dust kicked up behind the Métis as they spread out in search of their livestock. Their clothes and faces were smeared with grey mud. Their horses appeared painted as if for battle. The men's eyes were grim, showing the strain they had undergone.

Beneteau signaled for a parley and they came together in a circle.

"Remember, the Sioux set the fire to get something from us. They'll be after these animals, too," Beneteau said. "I think there is a creek ahead where those trees are growing. The horses may have forded the stream and holed up in those badlands," he added.

They rode forward in a spread–out formation until they converged at the small stream. The Métis plunged their horses into the water and came up dripping on the other side. One man raised his arm and circled it in the air; they drew toward him.

"That's where they went all right," Beneteau said when he saw the trail of hooves. The Métis slipped back into two columns of riders and rode forward at a canter.

"There in the rocks, Ti Jacques. Did you see it?"

High on a bluff, a sparkle as if from a chunk of mica had rippled just a little too much.

"I'd say it was a signal," Ti Jacques said.

The Métis continued until they rounded a bend and saw their animals huddled with their backs to a range of bluffs from which they could not escape.

"Okay, men, right up the middle and when the animals split, circle behind and drive them home. Ti Jacques, Jean Baptiste, we'll be the rear guard."

The Sioux were surprised by the maneuver. Horses and oxen came plunging at their concealed positions. When they jumped to flee, it scared the animals away from them and the Métis riders pushed past them. Had the Sioux numbered more than 20, they could have overpowered the Métis riders, but faced with the repeating fire power of the three–man rear guard, they could only follow sullenly at a distance while the Métis drove their property back to the wagon train.

Beneteau ordered a pair of oxen to be cut back and left for the warriors. As the beasts stood under the blaring sun, Beneteau rode Bronc in a circle around them, raised his Henry high in the sky and let loose a war cry that screeched over the prairie.

"The White Owl knows his brothers," he shouted in Sioux, then turned and rode after the others.

Beneteau and his riders were welcomed royally when they came upon the cart train, circled and ready for night camp. Without the extra horses and oxen, Henri Larocque would have been forced to call off the hunt.

After a quick report to Henri, Beneteau sought out Koohkoum Emma and Horace Throckmorton Bunny III.

The Medicine Man was conversing with Father Belgarde when Phillipe strode up to the campfire.

"Beans and coffee are on the fire, Hinhanska," said Horace when he saw Beneteau.

"Good evening, Father," Beneteau said to the priest. He got a plate and cup and helped himself, then collapsed on the ground, his back propped against one of the cart's high wheels. He ran his forearm across his brow and wolfed down the food.

"We've had quite a day," the priest said. "Don't forget to thank Our Lady and Jesus, Phillipe."

"Yes, Father," Beneteau said. "Who will you be thanking, Mr. Bunny?"

"I will be thanking the Creator," Horace said. "Not just for aid in the struggle with the Sioux, but for my Mandan heritage, which could have been used to avert most of this."

"That's what we were just discussing," said the priest.

“Horace says that we could have traded our way out of our bad day.”

“You mean we could have set up a trading post?” Beneteau said, his voice laced with sarcasm.

“Hinhanska, you know the Sioux depend on the land for survival,” Horace said.

“Horace said we wouldn’t have had a problem if we had shared some of our food with the Indians,” the priest said.

“They didn’t ask,” Beneteau said. “I gave them two ox back there.”

“Yes, but, Hinhanska, if you had given them some oxen and a few horses before today, this wagon train would have fared better. You know they have been watching us for some time.”

“You saw their signals, too,” Beneteau said.

“He may be right,” Father Belgarde said. “You gentlemen can discuss it. I have an evening prayer service at the campfire to attend.”

“I will go with you, Father,” said Koohkoum Emma. “Horace, can you take care of the kitchen?”

“Yes, I can handle it. And it will give me some time to educate Mr. Beneteau. Father Belgarde has told me how difficult religion can be among the Métis men.”

“See you, Father,” Beneteau said, nodding his head as the priest and Koohkoum left.

“Mr. Bunny, you are one sorry sight,” Beneteau said when they were alone. Horace Throckmorton Bunny III was still covered with mud. Only his hands were clean. The fire danced off the old man’s face and splotches of grey mingled with his dark skin reminded Phillipe Beneteau of a paint horse he used to have.

"You are not a pretty sight, either, Hinhanska. You must have scared the Sioux away. Just remember they are our brothers, too."

"We've met before," Beneteau said.

The old man busied himself with tidying up around the campfire. "You know, your grandmother and I are growing fond of each other," he said finally.

"That kind of scares me," Beneteau said, but inwardly he didn't mind. Koohkoum Emma had been alone for 10 years now. "You figure you might want to tie the knot?"

"We'd be inclined to just carry on so long as we're fit," Horace said.

"You'd be my grandpa, Mr. Bunny."

"That could be a burden I'd have to bear," the old man said. "She is a very good woman. Perhaps, no burden would be too great for such a prize."

"Well, you folks work it out," Beneteau said. He looked across the camp circle and watched as Maria Larocque climbed into their cart for the night. Henri was still smoking his pipe by the fire. Beneteau knew the wagon train leader would yet make his rounds to assure that the Métis were ready if anymore surprises were coming their way.

He decided to check on Bronc, who was picketed with the other buffalo runners between the wagons and night guards. He carried a small bag of oats with him and the horse nickered when he heard his footsteps. "Here you go, boy, a little something for you, too, after a long day." Beneteau fed the horse the oats from his hand, then stroked his back and rubbed his belly. "If I wasn't so damned tired, I'd stay out with you all night, Bronc," he said. There was a small pool of water nearby. Beneteau went to it, took off his clothes and waded into the water naked. The shock of the cold liquid on his body refreshed him, prompted him to think. He still missed Buster.

As he shook off and started to dress, he allowed that he might be falling in love himself. But Beneteau knew that Henri Larocque was a high–minded man and wanted only the best for his daughter. He didn't have much to offer except himself. Matter of fact, he was a wanted man.

Beneteau began to wonder what he'd do when this hunt was over. He wasn't much for trapping anymore. He wondered if he could be a cowboy.

He started at the sound of footsteps approaching in the dark as he finished dressing. Before he could react, he heard Ti Jacques's voice say, "Easy, Phillipe, it is just me, your old buddy."

"What keeps you up at this time of the night?" Beneteau said.

"I felt like having a pipe of tobacco," Ti Jacques said.

The two men sat squatted cross legged in the dark and passed a rawhide pouch between them and filled their pipes, then lit them and blew out smoke into the cool air.

"You know, Phillipe, I've been thinking hard about why French Louis would lie to the sheriff about you," Ti Jacques said.

"Yeh, it looks like I have yet another score to settle, Beneteau said. "What do you suppose got into that bastard?"

"I was cleaning my rifle tonight and when I went to my war bag to fetch some cleaning patches, I got near enough to Henri Larocque's fire to hear him talking to his daughter."

"Okay, so what did you hear? Did old Henri tell her to stay away from me?"

"Nah, it was worse than that, Phillipe. Henri was arguing with her. I heard him tell her that if French Louis asked for her hand in marriage, she should accept it. He would give her a good life and a position of prominence in the city of Devils Lake."

"What did Maria think of that?"

"She said that she would never be important because she is a half-breed woman and she told her father she didn't love French Louis. Henri said she was a fool."

"I'm the fool for trusting that son of a bitch," said Beneteau.

"When Maria started to cry, I got out of there. I thought you should know this."

"Ti Jacques," Beneteau said, "I'd trust you watching out for my backside anytime. And I will watch out for yours, too."

Beneteau walked over and patted Bronc once more before he joined his companion to return to the camp.

"You know," Beneteau said as they padded softly in the dark on their moccasins, "I don't think I've ever met a man with money you could even trust with your dog. By the time you got back, he'd have the dog trained to bite you."

"French Louis sure didn't gain much ground with Maria," Ti Jacques said.

"Aw, you know what I mean," said Beneteau.

"Phillipe, you only have one witness that you didn't kill that miner—old Mr. Bunny. And who is going to believe an old coot like him?"

"What's worse," Beneteau said. "It looks like he's going to be a relative."

A pair of camp dogs barked at the two men as they made their way through the entrance to the cart camp.

"I'll have to sleep on what you told me," Beneteau said.

"Tomorrow, Henri wants us out scouting for buffalo," Ti Jacques said. "See you in the morning."

Chapter 11

The three Métis riders sat at the brow of a hill in the breaking daylight and looked back through the sun's rays at their camp below. The carts were circled, smoke curled from campfires, the people were beginning to stir.

"Well, boys, it's up to us to find some buffalo—let's get going," said Beneteau. He reined Bronc's head to the west and nudged him into a canter.

"To the first four–legged," shouted Ti Jacques as he and Jean Baptiste sped past Beneteau and his mount.

And they were off, their mounts gleaming in the sunlight. Jean Baptiste and Ti Jacques had already gained a 50-yard advantage when Beneteau let his lanky piebald have a free rein. Beneteau screeched a war cry and his horse drew closer to the ground, his stride lengthened and the beat of the hooves echoed into the man's midsection.

Ahead, the other two mens' horses lunged forward. The speedy Métis runners would not be easy to overtake for they were also bred for endurance. Neither of the two racers bothered to look back at where Beneteau was positioned.

Beneteau worried that this boyish foolishness could deplete their horses' energies later in the day, but he, too, was carried away in the spirit of a good race.

From the corner of his left eye, Beneteau saw another horseman swing into view, bending low over the saddle and riding for all it was worth. He bent his head in the wind rushing past and was astonished to see the new rider was Maria Larocque. She wore a wide smile. Beneteau shook his head, but kept on racing.

Bronc was gaining on Ti Jacques and Jean Baptiste, but Maria was pushing her horse in close to Bronc's own rear.

A jackrabbit popped out of a clump of sage brush and the moment the forward riders crossed an imaginary line at the startled four–legged critter's hiding place, they pulled up. An antelope, a deer, a badger or even a skunk could have ended the race.

"That's one for you boys, but who won?" Beneteau said when he brought Bronc to a halt where they waited.

"I think I got him by a nose," Ti Jacques said.

"It was so close we should have had a judge," said Jean Baptiste.

"Maria, what in the hell are you doing out here?" said Beneteau.

She had ridden her horse right in the middle of their huddle.

"I just don't think men should have all the fun. And that was fun already. Phillipe Beneteau, I want you to let me scout with you guys," Maria said, with a wide, pearly smile, her dark eyes sparkling. She, like they, wore buckskin trousers, moccasins and a wool shirt. But no flat-brimmed hat, her long black hair, instead, simply tied neatly behind in a pony tail.

Beneteau was more worried about dealing with her father than having her along. He was confident she could ride with them. Her presence would, however, cause them extra concern. But who could turn down her charm?

“What do you think, boys? Willing to let her come or should we send her back to camp?”

“Gees, Phillipe,” said Jean Baptiste. “You are the headman. We have no quarrel with Henri.”

“You dumb moose,” said Ti Jacques. “She can ride better than you.”

“You, too,” said Jean Baptiste.

“Hold on, it isn’t a question of who can ride or shoot best,” said Beneteau.

“Then, what is it, Phillipe Beneteau? Afraid a woman will show you up?” said Maria. She stared directly into his hazel eyes.

Beneteau softened under her taunting gaze. “Okay, you can stay, but you have to be within eyesight of one of us.”

“Oh sure,” she said. “Like you won’t always be watching me anyway. Keep your mind on the buffalo, Phillipe Beneteau. I can take care of myself. You’ll see.”

“Does your father know where you are? He’ll probably come riding after us,” Beneteau said.

“I told Koohkoum Emma and Mr. Bunny that I would be with you guys scouting for buffalo. They will let him know not to worry.”

“A wily woman will think of everything,” Beneteau said. “All right, let’s keep going.” They urged their horses to a trot and aimed in a westerly direction again.

They had traveled half a day from camp when they came upon the first sign of buffalo. A threesome of wolves, a bitch and two half grown pups, fled from a buffalo calf carcass the animals had been feasting on. The kill was not fresh, but it was encouraging. Over the next hill they struck a worn trail that headed off to the northwest.

Beneteau weighed what to do. He decided to pair with Maria and follow the trail and put Jean Baptiste and Ti Jacques out as flankers in case the buffalo meandered.

"I know you don't need to be told, but remember that buffalo attract other hunters. Stay alert. Fire a signal if you see only buffalo. All other signals will be hand signs. We'll meet in the center unless someone runs into trouble. Maria, you will be the messenger back to your father if we are attacked. Otherwise, you ride with me and put those big dark eyes to work."

"Are we going to bring meat back to camp or just words?" Maria said.

"I could stand some fresh meat," said Ti Jacques.

"I'm hungry just thinking about it," said Jean Baptiste.

"Take a calf or a young cow," said Beneteau. "But we'll have to find them first. Keep your eyes and ears open. And don't forget to check the sky for our winged friends." The other two Métis riders slipped away and disappeared over the hill and Phillipe Beneteau and Maria were left alone.

They moved ahead and hung on each bend in the trail and Beneteau noticed that the old tracks had been imprinted by more recent travel. Maria estimated that there were not more than 50 buffalo in the bunch. The dark trail curved to the south ahead of them and behind a range of round hills. Maria broke from Beneteau's side and loped her horse to near the top of a hill. She dismounted and let her horse's reins dangle to the ground while she crept forward to the top.

Below her, Beneteau watched as she wiggled her way forward. The sensation of watching her in motion was always the same, only more so as she had blossomed into full womanhood. Damned woman, you can't tell her anything, he thought.

She had no more than peeked over the brow of the hill, than she turned quickly and slithered back to where she could stand. And then she waved to Beneteau and raised her hands to the side of her head and pointed her index fingers skyward, signaling buffalo.

Beneteau spurred Bronc toward her. By the time he got to Maria's position, she had her Winchester out of the scabbard and sat waiting for him to give the command.

"How far away are they?" he said in a low voice.

"Not more than a mile," she said.

"Then, we'll have to get closer before we run them," he said.

"I'm ready to run them right now," she said. She dug her heels into her horse's ribs and was off at a full gallop before Beneteau could reply.

She disappeared over the ridge top as Beneteau got Bronc into action and when they followed, Beneteau saw Maria was already plunging her horse recklessly down the other side.

At 750 yards, the alarmed buffalo had split and were in full motion away from the riders.

"Too soon, damn it, too soon," Beneteau muttered. He was forced to trail Maria and the group of buffalo she was charging. And he was forced to admit that the buffalo were outdistancing them. He eased back on Bronc and watched the dark brown shaggy shapes bob and spread the distance between them and Maria. He didn't think she would ever stop, but finally she pulled her horse up, too.

"Aw god, Phillipe, I'm sorry," she said when he rode up. "I know better. I thought we had them."

"We've all made that mistake," Beneteau said. "We should be happy that we've found some buffalo. We'll pick up their trail again."

They heard a shot ahead of them and continued on to find Jean Baptiste with a young buffalo cow down.

"They ran right into me," he said when Beneteau and Maria rode up.

"You've saved the day," Beneteau said. He and Maria jumped from their horses to help Jean Baptiste prop the buffalo up on its belly. While Jean Baptiste, ran his skinning knife down the buffalo's back to open the hide, Beneteau cut the beast's tongue out. Maria gathered chips and dried brush for a cooking fire.

"I better ride out and locate Ti Jacques," Beneteau said after wrapping the tongue in a piece of hide. "He's as hungry for fresh meat as the rest of us."

Beneteau was sitting at the edge of a clump of buffalo berry bushes when he saw four riders loping his way. He recognized Ti Jacques, but didn't realize one of the others was Henri Larocque until they were passing within a quarter mile of where he sat.

"Uh, oh, old Henri's going to have a kitten," he said, putting Bronc to a trot toward the men.

"You worthless pig," Henri shouted at Beneteau. "What have you done with my daughter? If she's been hurt I'll kill you." Henri quirted his horse right at Beneteau and lashed out at his face with the whip.

Beneteau grabbed the quirt and dove at Henri, knocking him from his horse to the ground. When the two men regained their feet, both were still holding the quirt. Henri's companions were on the ground now and tried to separate them.

"Hold on there, Henri. She's okay. She didn't want to go back," Beneteau said, trying to calm the older man.

Ti Jacques hung on Beneteau's right arm, just in case he decided to swing at Henri. They got the whip out of Henri's hand and pulled the two apart. Henri glowered at Beneteau.

"For God's sake, Henri, she wanted to scout buffalo, so we let her come along. She's up ahead with Jean Baptiste skinning out a buffalo right now."

"Damn you, Phillipe Beneteau," Henri said. "Damn you to hell. Let go of my arms and I'll tear the no good in half."

"Now, now there Henri, just get back on your horse and we'll catch up with her and Jean Baptiste. I think Phillipe will be scouting for more buffalo and we don't want to keep him from his work," said Ti Jacques.

Beneteau took the cue and grabbed Bronc and left. "Morning, Henri," he said, touching his hand to his hat brim as he passed by Maria's father. He thought he knew real good where Maria got her temper. He could still hear Henri cursing as he and Bronc rode out of sight over a hill.

The first shot Beneteau heard sounded like the report of a small cannon. It was he knew the signature of a .50 caliber Sharps—a white buffalo hunter's tool. In all, Beneteau counted 10 shots before he rode within view of the small bunch of buffalo. Two men lay at the brow of a small rise on the prairie, their rifles propped on tripods fashioned from sticks. It was obvious they had used a dry creek bed to gain their position down wind of the herd. The buffalo stood grazing nearby their companions who lie where they fell on the prairie grass.

Another beast dropped at the report of still another shot. Beneteau saw only two horses staked in the dry coulee. At that, he knew these hunters planned only to take the tongues and hides in the wasteful practice of the white sports hunter.

Overcome by his anger, he spurred Bronc and headed toward the remaining buffalo. At his approach, the bulls raised their tails in alarm, turned the remaining cows and charged away from him.

Beneteau then made a half circle and charged the white men.

The two men stood up and threw their hands in the air.

"Nicht schiessen, nicht schiessen," one of the hunters yelled. He was a round man wearing tanned riding britches tucked into shiny, black boots. His companion was a weathered cowboy in a crumpled grey Stetson. He wore Levis and a Colt hung from a cartridge belt slung around his waist.

"Yeh, mister," he said as Beneteau rode up to them. "Don't shoot. We're just having a little sport."

Beneteau stepped off Bronc and led him to the two men. His right hand hung free if he should need his own gun.

"Howdy, Curly's my name," the cowboy said, extending his hand. "This is Baron von Stranski from Germany. He's paid me a month's range wages to take him out for a buffalo hunt."

Beneteau eyed the two suspiciously before returning the handshake.

"Guten Tag, Guten Tag," the big German said. He shook Beneteau's hand with both of his. "Indianer?" he inquired of the cowboy.

"Nope," the cowboy said, shaking his head sideways. "But I think we ought to give him the damned buffalo if he wants them." The Baron obviously didn't understand what he said.

He shrugged. “What’d you get all excited about?” the cowboy said to Beneteau.

Beneteau explained that he was scouting for a Métis hunting party that had carts and they would take all the buffalo for hides and meat. “Buffalo are getting damned hard to find these days,” he said.

“Well, maybe we can make a deal,” the cowboy said. “His royal highness here just wants a hide and skull for trophies and to eat some buffalo tongue.”

Beneteau said his people would welcome getting the buffalo.

The big German’s eyes showed concern. The cowboy said, “It’ll be okay—you got it—okay?”

“Okay, okay, gut,” the German said. While the two hunters packed away their big rifles in saddle scabbards, Beneteau rode to where the buffalo were scattered and began cutting the animals’ throats to allow them to bleed. He figured the other Métis couldn’t be far away and they would need some carts, as well.

“I’ll ride for help,” he told the cowboy when he and the German approached.

“You do what you have to,” Curly said. “We may still be here when you get back but his royal highness wants to shoot an antelope and a big horn sheep. Maybe even a bear or a wolf.” The cowboy carried a canvas bag into which he tossed a tongue before he set to work skinning a bull he had rolled on its back. The German signaled he would like to eat some of the meat and it looked like he meant right now.

“Aw, buffalo shit, I don’t know how the hell I got into this deal,” the cowboy mumbled as he dropped his work to gather some fire wood.

Beneteau was right. The other Métis were finishing the work of packaging the meat from the cow downed by Jean Baptiste when he rode up on them. The red meat was stacked in the center of the hide, which was folded over and tied with tendons from the animals' legs. Henri Larocque was talking to the workers, but went silent at the sight of Beneteau.

"Henri's calmed down a little but I guess he isn't over it yet," Ti Jacques warned Beneteau in a low voice.

Maria stood by her father and cast only a side glance at Beneteau before he spoke without dismounting.

"I've got about 10 more buffalo down a few miles from here," Beneteau said. "Came across some sports hunters who offered the fresh kills. They only want some tongue meat and a buffalo hide, but they shot a lot more than they needed."

"Henri has already sent for the carts," Jean Baptiste said. "Right, Henri?"

"I planned to make camp here tonight," Henri said, "but I'm sure we can make it a few more miles for some buffalo. We'll continue on to them."

They set out with Beneteau riding ahead, followed by Jean Baptiste, Ti Jacques, Henri, Maria and the other Métis hunter whose companion was the messenger sent to the carts.

The cowboy was roasting a big chunk of buffalo hump when they rode up. "Help yourself," he told the Métis. "Better get some quick before Herr Big Ass here eats everything. He calls me Herr Curly. Ain't that some handle?"

The baron had a hunk of the the meat in his left hand and carved chunks of it with his hunting knife. "Gut, gut, auch gut," he said.

"Anybody here understand that crap?" Curly said. "I only understand him when he says something is good. We had an interpreter when this started but he got scared out after we got on the plains. His royalty thinks this is great near as I can tell."

Beneteau said they would eat after they cleaned up the buffalo and he loped Bronc to a fat cow that had been downed. Behind him, he could hear Henri giving orders. The others fanned out to the different carcasses and the processing began.

The baron came down from the hilltop to watch. He clucked "gut," and "schoen" and "wunderbar," as he watched Beneteau remove his animal's hide with deft strokes of his knife.

Beneteau tossed the German a chunk of the liver when he opened and gutted the cow. "Try this," he said.

The German caught the meat, and shrugged.

"Like this," Beneteau said and he bit into a chunk of the bloody liver, still warm from the animal's body. "It will make you a better hunter," Beneteau told the German.

The baron grimaced slightly, but bit into the meat, then his face squinched up and he spat it out, "Schlecht, das Fleisch schmeckt wie Scheisse," he said.

"Taste like shit, huh?" said Beneteau, who only knew that one word in German. He took another bite of the liver and went back to cutting off the legs on his buffalo, which he had rolled on its back on the hide.

Beneteau felt pretty good with getting some meat and hides. Not much, but it was a start and the rest of the Métis would appreciate the fresh meat. He looked over and saw Maria sawing away on a buffalo. Henri made his way around encouraging their work, but he stayed away from Beneteau. "Nothing in the world like hitting it off with the father of the woman you love," he mumbled to himself. "Old Henri must have his sights set on French Louis' money." Maria looked over at him quickly, then dropped her gaze when he caught her.

In the distance, the screeching wheels of the cart train revealed their approach, then they wobbled into sight on the horizon. Some of the outriders were loping their horses in front of the carts.

Henri waited for them with his hands on his hips. The baron stood at his side, shading his eyes to watch the Métis approach.

"Leiterwagen," said the German.

Henri directed the carts to form a circle and set up camp. The women fashioned tripods from which they hung cast–iron pots for rendering fat. Part of the band waded into the business of finishing butchering the buffalo. Intestines were rolled out of the beasts and hearts and livers separated along with paunches. Tongues were tossed on hides, as were cuts from the humps and loins.

After the meat was cut and stowed on hides, it was loaded on carts and taken to the camp, where women sliced the meat into thin strips which they laid across drying racks. What wasn't dried was tossed into the rendering pots. The camp wreaked with the tantalizing odor of meat cooking. Someone signaled a lone cart and three riders were approaching on the horizon with the cow downed by Jean Baptiste.

The Métis camp fires brightened as the sun sank slowly out of sight and someone broke out a fiddle. Henri opened a wine cask from which the men and women drew cups of grape wine. When the adults weren't watching, small boys rushed to the cask, filled their cups and disappeared under the nearest cart to watch men and women kick up dust with their jigging.

Beneteau stood by the cowboy Curly, who was expressionless during the entire celebration.

"What are you thinking?" Beneteau said.

"I'm thinking if that big, fat bastard took a real likin' to you folks, I could go back to wrangling cows," said Curly.

"Or you could hang along with us and have some fun hunting," Beneteau said.

Curly smiled and took out a sack of tobacco and some yellow rice cigarette papers. "Care for a smoke?" he asked Beneteau, then handed him the sack and papers.

"You mean you wouldn't mind if we tagged along?" he said, blowing off a cloud of smoke.

"We're a friendly people," Beneteau said. "Besides, it looks like there isn't going to be much hunting like this in the future. Everybody is killing buffalo these days. We've made a living hunting for years, but I'm afraid it's about over."

"What do you plan to do?" Curly said.

"I don't know," Beneteau said. He flicked the ashes from the end of his smoke, then wet it at the seams with his tongue again to hold it together. "From what I've seen, it looks like the cattle coming in are replacing the buffalo. Maybe I'll be a cowboy."

"Even that's changing fast," said Curly. "Damn settlers are fencing off the range. Some cattlemen are staking out ranches. It's their only chance."

"How about you?" said Beneteau. "You going to be a rancher?"

"Nah," said Curly. "I've worked cattle since I was a kid in Texas. But I never wanted to be the big boss. Ties you down. Can't read much and hate to write. But I can read a horse or a cow."

"I guess I can read the buffalo and the wind," said Beneteau. He thought to himself that he was right about cowboys. They weren't much different than he was.

In the firelight, the two men watched Henri Larocque and the baron clap their hands to the music as the fiddlers sawed and the dancers twirled in their own dust.

Two weeks on the trail and the Métis buffalo hunters had managed to butcher 11 buffalo, barely enough meat to feed themselves for a couple of months.

Still, they were happy tonight under the great star-filled sky, their campfires joining in the dance to the fiddle music.

Chapter 12

Phillipe Beneteau's knife blade whispered back and forth at him as he honed it on the sharpening stone. He watched the prone shapes of Horace Throckmorton Bunny III and Koohkoum Emma stir under their blankets where they had spent the night together. Beneteau couldn't put his finger on what it was that troubled him by the sight.

"Hinhanska, you are readying yourself for another day of adventure," the old man said when he slipped into the morning air and his baggy trousers.

Koohkoum Emma avoided her grandson's eyes and busied herself immediately with tending the fire and boiling water for coffee.

"Actually, I was just thinking of the joy I had in taking off the balls of that old buffalo bull yesterday," Beneteau said.

The old man poked his head through his cloak and his brown eyes fixed on Beneteau's face when the last of his grey mane emerged.

"You seem to be upset that your grandmother and I have shared our bed," Horace said. "You shouldn't be. We have decided to share our lives."

"Nah, Mr. Bunny, that's not it. Having you for a grandpa is about the joy I'd have had to roast a few steaks from the old bull and enjoy the meat."

"I may end my days not being able to tell if it was the gentle care of your grandmother or the Christian religion that ruined you. You have not learned yet, Hinhanska, that your way and my way are the Creator's way. Whatever blessing He brings in a new day are gifts from the Above. Take a deep breath and thank your Creator for life, Hinhanska. He has been very generous with us two–leggeds."

"I've been taught that already," said Beneteau. "But I have also been taught that when two people come together for life, they should be married by a preacher. You should have Father Belgarde tie the knot."

Koohkoum Emma ignored the conversation, but soon handed each of the men coffee from the blackened pot hanging on a metal tripod over the fire. Then, she cut slabs of meat from a chunk of roasted buffalo and put it and fried bread on their plates.

The two men busied themselves with eating and said no more. Beneteau tested the sharpness of his knife and it sliced through the meat as if it had been a hunk of back lard from the beast. Horace sawed his meat into small pieces to accommodate his lack of teeth.

"What are your plans today?" Horace said finally.

Beneteau already knew that he and his two companions would be out scouting for more buffalo again. "We've got a lot more buffalo hunting to do before this is over," he said, rising to leave. "Think about what I said, Mr. Bunny," he said. Then he left for where Bronc was picketed.

He heard the footsteps coming up lightly behind him before he turned and saw her.

"Good morning, Phillipe Beneteau," Maria said.

"I hope you aren't planning to join us today," he said.

"My father said I was never to do that again," she said. "He also said he didn't want to see me with you."

"You picked a fine way to obey him," Beneteau said. Maria stood straight in the morning sun rising behind her and Beneteau saw the roundness of her hips silhouetted below her slim waist. He didn't need to see her eyes and he sure didn't need to listen to the beat of her heart beneath her bosom. He was surprised he didn't get tongue tied already.

"Take this for luck," she said, thrusting her red neckerchief into his hand. Before he could reply, she turned and walked quickly back to camp. Beneteau held the cloth to his nose and drew in a deep breath, then silently thanked his Creator and God for the day. Bronc nuzzled his back and brought him back to realty.

He got the horse saddled and bridled and was about to swing up on him to limber him for the day when Ti Jacques and Jean Baptiste arrived with Curly.

"We're going to have company today," Ti Jacques said.

"Yep, I hope you don't mind our tagging along," said Curly. "Your boss Henri has hit it off pretty good with Herr Big Ass. He'll be coming, too."

Beneteau had one thought before he spoke. Maybe he had been a little hasty in thanking God for the day. "Can he ride?"

"Oh yeah," said Curly. "He can ride and he can shoot. He just don't know a damned thing and keeps asking questions all day."

"We'll try to put Jean Baptiste with him. He loves to explain things, right Jean Baptiste?" Beneteau said.

"Yeah," the big man said. Actually, the Métis were fascinated by the big German and thought kindly toward him for his gift of the buffalo.

They cut their horses from the herd, then saddled and led Baron von Stranski's high–stepping grey back to camp. Beneteau noticed the saddle was flat as a pancake and the stirrups were metal. It looked like a flimsy little contraption. But attached to the saddle was a rifle scabbard and it looked like it might work.

The baron, wearing his riding britches, shiny black boots and a fur hat perched over a fringed jacket was ready when they showed up. The German stood on the hub of a wagon wheel to mount while Curly held the animal at the bridle.

"Gut, gut, wir gehen, schnell," the big German told them.

"You show the baron a good day," Henri Larocque told them, but he spoke at Ti Jacques and Jean Baptiste when he did.

"We'll take care of him, Henri," Beneteau said.

Henri shook the big German's hand and wished him good luck.

"Vielen Dank, vielen Dank," the German said.

"No racing today," Beneteau said. "Not until we at least find out if he can stay on that pancake." And then they were off in search of more buffalo. The weather was kicking up and it looked like a squall was coming in from the northwest.

Curly rode beside Beneteau and the baron rode between Ti Jacques and Jean Baptiste.

"You'll be surprised at how well Big Ass does for as little as he knows," the cowboy said. "He potted an antelope at 500 yards with that boom stick he carries. He doesn't look like he could find his butt with both hands."

Beneteau looked back over his shoulder and watched the big German keep rhythm with his horse's trot. The German smiled and raised his right arm bent at the elbow and fingers extended skyward as a greeting. "Waidmann's Heil," the German said.

"It's too damned bad somebody doesn't know what he's talking about," Curly said.

"I think I know," said Beneteau. "I feel the same way. We're moving and that always makes the day better. I think he's wishing us good hunting."

They were on the wide buffalo trail which carried fresh tracks again when the thunderstorm hit. There was no place to take cover, so they draped their bedrolls around their shoulders, bowed their heads and kept going.

The first wind gusts blew fine dust that peppered their faces and hands. The horses leaned into the wind's strength and wobbled when it let up. Lightning cracked overhead followed by the grumble of thunder. As the wind subsided, rain fell. The air grew still and the rain built up until it was beating them with a torrent. Beneteau called a halt when he could no longer see where he was going and the five men dismounted and huddled in a small circle.

"Wunderbar, shoen, das ist gut," said the baron, rainwater cascading down his cheeks.

"The crazy bastard is enjoying this," Curly said. A current poured off the brim of his cowboy hat. The baron's fur hat looked like a drowned rat but his face was split by a wide grin.

"Krazee bassdard, ja gut," he said.

Beneteau was thinking that the buffalo trail was being washed out. They would be back to the first step of finding a fresh trail when the squall blew through. And it did shortly. The grass was flattened in spots and water gushed down gullies. The trail they had been on was a sea of mud.

"We might as well take some time to dry out," Beneteau said. The sky lightened overhead and the sun peeked through clouds.

"I've gone through this with a herd of cattle," said Curly. "It's a real mess trying to get them back together. I kind of like this buffalo hunting right now."

The big German produced a flask of whiskey which he offered to the others.

Each took a pull. Beneteau felt his insides warm immediately. The German was okay, he thought.

Ti Jacques gulped a huge swallow.

The big German grinned. "Ist gut?" He threw his arms around Ti Jacques. "Comrades, nicht wahr?"

Ti Jacques took another big pull on the flask and it made its way around the group again.

The German began to sing. "In Muenchen steht ein Hofbraeuhaus, eins, zwei, gsuffa."

As the liquor took over, they all began to come in under the German's direction to the refrain, "eins, zwei, gsuffa."

They laughed and plopped down in the mud encircled by their horses. Ti Jacques tilted the flask back one last time and tapped it to extract the last drop, then fell backward.

Beneteau tied Bronc's rein to his wrist and closed his eyes to catch a nap. When he awoke, Curly was up leading the baron's horse and his own to patches of grass that were still popping back from being laid over by the rain.

He nudged Jean Baptiste and Ti Jacques and they, too, took their mounts to grass.

“What in hell was that stuff?” Jean Baptiste said.

“I don’t know,” said Ti Jacques. “I don’t remember the end.”

“I suppose old Henri will blame me for this, too,” Beneteau said. “Well, the baron is one helluva buffalo hunter.”

When, they had finished letting their horses get some grass and kicked loose the mud from their pants and boots, Beneteau got everyone mounted and came up with a plan to have the four spread out a quarter mile of each other to pick up the trail. He would sweep beyond their line with a circle. One shot would signal buffalo, two trouble. They would meet at the center of the line before the sunset.

He set Bronc to a canter to put distance between him and the others, then slowed him to a trot when he was out. His plan was to make a circle that started on the north, curved west, south and east and come up on the others from behind their line of march. No buffalo in that area meant a long day ahead tomorrow.

It was midmorning when Beneteau heard the single shot far off to the south. He pointed Bronc at the sound and gave him a loose rein. The piebald responded by stretching his long limbs into the distance gobblers that both he and the man seemed to enjoy so much. Beneteau was bent low over his neck when he saw the other four men bunched on a hilltop.

“Jean Baptiste spotted them,” Ti Jacques said before Beneteau got Bronc stopped. The piebald pranced, snorted and sidestepped, even as Beneteau reined him into a circle to bring his eagerness under control.

“How many, Jean Baptiste and where?” Beneteau said.

"Just over the next rise, Phillipe," Jean Baptiste said. There's a small flat. There must be at least 150."

"How do you boys propose to get them?" Curly said.

"We'll walk our horses at them until they get uncomfortable," Beneteau said. "Each man will pick a target and on my signal—we're off." He pulled his Henry from it's scabbard and rested the butt on his right thigh and they advanced. The baron, following their lead, unsheathed his .50 caliber Sharps. Silently, they rode toward the next hill, spread out about 25 yards apart.

They were downwind of the herd when they came into view. Below them nibbling prairie grass 500 yards away were the buffalo. The baron bounced off his horse and sat down, bringing his big gun to aim, but Beneteau was off Bronc and waving the German to stop before he got off his first shot.

"Don't shoot yet," Beneteau said. Then, he signed horses running and he raised his arms to show him aiming at a buffalo. Crude as it was, the German understood.

Beneteau boosted the big man back on his mount and they slowly edged toward the herd, only their horses' bits jingling softly to the creak of leather as they made their way to the buffalo.

The bulls were the first to react, raising their dark, shaggy heads in alarm. Tails up, small, dark eyes glistening in the sun, they crowded the cows and calves into a tight group, then watched sullenly as the riders neared.

Beneteau had been schooled on how to keep anyone from breaking out to be the first to make a kill. He knew they would get more buffalo if they charged as one in close. Too often, when the hunters bolted on their own, the fastest riders drove the beasts away from the other hunters and only a few buffalo were taken.

At 150 yards, the buffalo grew more alarmed with each step

the horses took. Beneteau raised his Henry and dropped it forward like a lance. Bronc exploded. So hard did he charge that the wind currents clouded Beneteau's eyes with tears. Bronc, unguided, singled out a cow and drove toward her. A bull whirled and charged. Beneteau, guiding Bronc with his knees now, dodged right and laid the bull over with a shot to the great animal's chest. The bull crumbled to its knees and Beneteau kept Bronc driving to the cow he had selected. He touched off another shot and it fell. Then he was in the midst of them. Another cow emerged in front of Bronc and Beneteau fired, knocking her down. He could hear the others shooting.

Beneteau saw the baron towering over the backs of the buffalo and heard the boom of the Sharps. A bull slammed into the ribs of the German's grey and Beneteau saw the big man topple, his left foot stuck in the metal stirrup. The grey bucked in fear as the German's leg followed his body over the right side. Beneteau saw the man's riding boot bouncing at the level of the horse's back before it disappeared with the jerking strides of the frightened horse. The horse plunged further into the center of the stampeding herd until he was loose from the man's body somewhere underneath the hooves of the buffalo.

Jean Baptiste had seen it from the other side and both he and Beneteau spurred their horses to where the German had gone down. By the time they got there, the last of the buffalo were fleeing with the German's horse running off riderless in the opposite direction.

"Catch that horse," Beneteau yelled to Ti Jacques, just as he swung down from Bronc to kneel by the side of the German. The man was still, the right side of his face crushed and his entire right side flattened as if hit by a huge boulder.

Curly dismounted 25 yards away and retrieved the Sharps, which had a cracked stock and was half covered by dirt. Then he rode to the baron's body.

"Damn," Curly said when he saw the baron.

"I'm afraid he's gone," said Beneteau

"Gone and then some," said Curly.

"You know, you couldn't tell him anything about being careful. He just seemed bent on doing whatever in the hell he pleased."

Ti Jacques returned with the grey in tow and Jean Baptiste retrieved the riding saddle, it's flimsy, pleasure-riding cinch torn loose at the buckle. They took the bedroll the baron had tied with thongs on the front of his saddle and rolled it out on the ground. Curly and Beneteau hoisted the big man onto the canvas while Ti Jacques and Jean Baptiste held it at the ends; then they folded it around the body and tied it.

"What are we going to do with the buffalo?" Jean Baptiste said.

"You and Ti Jacques take care of them," Beneteau said. "I'll ride with Curly back to our camp with the baron. I'll have Henri send the carts."

The men lifted the body to the back of the grey and secured it with their braided lariats. Then, Beneteau and the cowboy set off for the camp.

By Beneteau's reckoning, the camp couldn't be more than 15 miles away.

"What are your plans now?" Beneteau said to Curly.

"I reckon I'll take his body back to Medora, then get me another job wrangling cattle," the cowboy said.

"We have a service with a priest on the plains and bury our dead right out here when we lose a hunter," Beneteau said.

"That'd be nice," Curly said. "But I'd have to spend the rest of my life explaining what happened to the German. As it is, I got a tall bit of explaining to do. Maybe I will get me a small spread of my own off the confluence of the Missouri and Yellowstone rivers in Montana when I get this mess cleaned up."

Beneteau knew the region. The Métis hunted the area and traded at Fort Buford. He thought the land was controlled by the Sioux, who shared the buffalo with other hunters when there were plenty. "I didn't know the land was open to settlement," he said.

"Pretty damn near everything is open to some kind of settlement," Curly said. "If you are tough enough to take over a piece of ground, it's yours. I could have enough money coming from the baron to buy a few head of cattle and start up."

Beneteau's thoughts trailed off to the thought that the Métis had been hunting for two weeks and hadn't got more than 25 head. After getting Curly and the baron taken care of, he and the others would pick up the trail of the buffalo again, hoping for a larger herd. Something sure as hell wasn't going right on this hunting trip.

The two men were a grim sight, riding into the Métis camp with the baron's body draped over the grey horse. A group of women, children and men gathered to meet them. Henri Larocque stood at the head of the assembly.

"Now what have you done?" he demanded when Beneteau and Curly pulled up.

"We got into a bunch of buffalo and the baron's horse bucked him off and he was trampled," Beneteau said. "He's dead."

"My god," Henri said. "You can't do anything right. This man was our guest. He promised to come visit us in the Turtle Mountains. He even said he would make us a loan of money to help our people get land." He lunged at Beneteau and Bronc shied out of his reach. "Damn you to hell, Phillipe Beneteau."

Beneteau gave the reins of the grey to Curly, spun his horse and trotted off 20 yards before whirling the big piebald. "Take care of your boss," Beneteau said to the cowboy, who sat quietly through the argument. Curly just nodded. Beneteau then told Henri, "There are a dozen buffalo waiting to be butchered about 15 miles back due west. I will continue to look for more but my days of following you are over."

He reined Bronc and urged him to a full gallop away from the cart camp. In the wind he heard Henri's voice shouting, "Good, good, you damned scoundrel."

Pompous bastard, Beneteau thought to himself. He hadn't seen Maria but he could feel the lump of her kerchief pressed against his chest in his shirt pocket. He wanted to check on Koohkoum Emma and Horace but there wasn't time. If they had any problems he was sure someone would relay their message to him. He let Bronc run himself out before he slowed down. The anger he felt at Henri Larocque's bad mind was slower to subside but Beneteau had it under control by the time he topped the rise above where the buffalo lay scattered on the flat. Ti Jacques and Jean Baptiste had several of the beasts skinned and wrapped in their hides.

Without speaking, Beneteau took his own knife and began the grisly job of cutting the meat free. His knife slid through the membranes holding the animal's carcass to its shaggy hide. The Métis worked fast to get the meat cooled to prevent spoilage. If the carts didn't arrive, all three hunters could trim the chunks of buffalo into drying strips that would later be pounded and mixed with berries and buffalo bone marrow to make pemmican. Like their Indian brothers, the Métis wasted as little as possible. But they did not utilize everything unless they weren't on the move.

They could see the dust of the meat carts coming on the horizon by the time they had all the buffalo butchered. Beneteau told his two companions what happened and appointed Jean Baptiste as liaison. Ti Jacques volunteered to stay with Beneteau. They bagged a buffalo hump and rode into the west before Henri's group arrived.

That night Beneteau and Ti Jacques found a brush covered cave in a hillside for their camp. They had not come on more buffalo but late in the day they had signaled to a lone rider they took to be Jean Baptiste. He knew their general location in case they were needed. They felt secure enough to keep a small fire on which they roasted some of their meat on willow sticks.

"Henri seems to be going loco," Ti Jacques told Beneteau across the fire sparking between them.

"He has a lot on his mind," Beneteau allowed.

"Do you remember when we were kids and got caught bucking his milk cows? He was always a horse's ass. We were just kids and he wanted to beat us."

"The people say he takes after his father," Beneteau said. He wiped his knife blade on his pant leg and tossed the bone he was chewing in the fire. "His father was a full blooded Frenchman. Wanted to make a lot of money and get a big fancy house in Montreal. I suppose that Henri wants to be somebody, too," Beneteau said.

"But you wouldn't think he would blame us for the German getting killed by buffalo. Henri asked us to take him along."

"I think he was blaming me," Beneteau said. "He wants to make me look bad to everyone—especially Maria. Who knows, maybe he's right. Maybe I'm not the man for her. Maybe French Louis is. What are you going to do when this hunt is over?" Beneteau said, changing the subject.

"I don't know Phillipe, but we sure ain't going to feed our faces hunting buffalo. What are you thinking?"

"I'm thinking that cowboy Curly said a man could get a few cows and start ranching in this country if he was tough enough. I think if we can hunt buffalo, we could handle a few cows. Still care to throw in with me?"

Phillipe, I'd hang with you if we just went trapping skunks for a living. We go back a few years, don't we? You and me and old Jean Baptiste. Maybe we could raise horses, too—eh?"

"We'd have to have horses," Beneteau said. The fire was dying so he chucked another stick on it and sparks spiraled upward, then died. An uneasiness crept over Beneteau and he suggested he would take the first watch. He flicked back the hammer on the Army Colt and rolled its cylinder from habit, then reached for the Henry.

Beneteau was already rolling across the ground when the report of a rifle fired at close range reached his ear. In the corner of his eye he saw the distorted face of Ti Jacques as the bullet ripped into his head.

More shots followed and dust sprayed against his face. Beneteau continued to roll into the darkness. He slapped off a pair of shots with the Colt at the muzzle blasts that followed his movement, then he sprinted to where the horses were staked. Beneteau bridled Bronc and leapt on his back, urging him to full speed into the darkness. When they were out of range, he brought the piebald to an uneasy rest, then stroked his neck to quiet him. In the distance he heard cursing. He judged the attackers to be only two men and the hair bristled at the back of his neck when he guessed at who it was.

"I got one of them half breed bastards, Cal," Beneteau heard a man's voice say. "But the son of a bitch we're after gave us the slip again."

"We'll get him in the morning. He can't run far enough that we won't get him sooner or later."

Beneteau knew in the blackness of the night and the sorrow of his heart that he would be running no where. This time the attackers had come at him on his home ground. It was the very reason that he and Ti Jacques had relaxed their guard.

He reined Bronc around and prepared to charge the two men when he heard a voice shout. “You men see anything?”

Another answered, “Nah, the bastard slipped past us, Cal.”

Beneteau checked Bronc and slid off his back. With reins in hand, he silently led the horse in the dark until they were out of sight and earshot of the camp. Now, he knew he was up against at least three but most likely more.

Chapter 13

Beneteau found a flat rock in a washout and tied Bronc to it, then crouched and started toward where he was camped with Ti Jacques.

Rage riled his thinking. These white men were hunting him like he was a damned jackrabbit. Now, one of his best friends was dead. Nearing the camp, he heard a man clear his throat and spit.

"Keep your eyes peeled out there, Blackie," a voice shouted from where the fire still glowed against the brush. "This bastard we got ain't dead yet. But he will be."

"I got you covered," the dark form looming before Beneteau answered. Beneteau could make out the outline of the guard's head staring into the night. With catlike grace, Beneteau leapt at him and before the man could turn, he silenced him by slamming the butt of the Henry into the side of his neck. The form crumpled, a whiskey tainted breath escaping with his last gasp.

Beneteau stepped over the body and raced on, his moccasins barely scraping the ground. Through the brush, he saw three men standing over Ti Jacques.

"I'll finish the son of a bitch off," one said. Beneteau recognized the man called Cal and his bushy–faced friend in the glow of the fire. The one who had spoken pulled back the hammer on his revolver and pointed it at Ti Jacques, lying motionless on the ground. Beneteau aimed the Henry from his hip and a slug sped into the man's chest, hurling him backward out of the light of the campfire. The other two men turned and ran. Beneteau followed but instead of pursuing them, he hoisted Ti Jacques over his shoulders and retreated back to where he had Bronc tied. Halfway, he heard the attackers open fire on the camp again. He counted firing from four different guns. Beneteau located Bronc and boosted Ti Jacques over his withers then rolled up on the piebald's back. He found the North Star and set the horse to a gentle trot headed toward the east where the Métis would be.

Beneteau could feel the wetness from Ti Jacques's bleeding against his right leg. He tied Maria's neckerchief around his friend's head, hoping it would stem the flow of blood. His body was limp and Beneteau could not even tell because of the motion of the horse whether Ti Jacques breathed.

"Hold on," was all he could muster. "Hold on if you can." Beneteau thought about praying. Instead, he took the cross that hung around his neck and put it on Ti Jacques.

The sun was breaking in the east when the Métis camp wavered into view like a mirage. Beneteau cradled Ti Jacques's bloody head in his right arm. He inspected the wound and found the bullet had taken a chunk out of Ti Jacques's neck, not his head, but he had lost a lot of blood. Beneteau rode in silence past the people who came out to meet them. He pulled Bronc up at the fire of Koohkoum Emma and Horace Throckmorton Bunny III.

The two old people helped slide Ti Jacques off the horse and onto a blanket on the ground. Beneteau explained what had happened while Emma cleaned the wound. Before she bandaged it, Horace mixed a paste from his medicine bag which he daubed on the gash. Then, Horace touched warm water to the lips of Ti Jacques whose eyes opened into slits before he groaned and fell back into a coma.

"Will he be okay?" Beneteau said.

"We'll have him ready for buffalo hunting real soon," the old Medicine Man said. "It will take more than lead to do away with this young man."

Before Beneteau could leave, Henri Larocque showed up.

"Trouble follows you like a pack of dogs after a bitch in heat," Henri said.

Beneteau fought down the urge to hit Henri. "Take care of my friend, Henri," was all he said. He brushed past him and hoisted himself back on Bronc and they slowly left the camp behind. Before they had gone a quarter mile, Jean Baptiste galloped up beside them.

"I don't know where you are going," the big guy said, "but I'm going with you."

"Thanks, Jean Baptiste. I'd say you know where I am going. These white bastards have pushed me far enough. Now they have brought my friends into it."

"How many of them are there?" Jean Baptiste said.

"At least four."

"Do you think we can catch them?"

"I think so, but Bronc and I are going to need a bit of rest first. He hasn't had anything to eat or drink all night. We'll head back to our camp and start from there. I hope those bastards didn't run off with my saddle."

Beneteau was right about one thing. The attackers didn't hang around. He and Jean Baptiste circled the camp and found their trail leading south. Jean Baptiste said he'd stand guard while Beneteau hobbled Bronc on some prairie grass and got some rest. When Beneteau came back to the camp site, he found his saddle perched on the ground just as he had left it. His surprise assault apparently scared the attackers enough so that they didn't even rifle the saddlebags.

He plopped down on the ground and using the saddle as a pillow, he fell asleep.

The big hand of Jean Baptiste shook him back to reality. "We've got visitors again, "Jean Baptiste said quietly. A dozen Sioux on painted war ponies sat near the Métis horses.

Beneteau shook off his drowsiness and reached for his Henry. Jean Baptiste already stood at his side, his rifle in hand.

"What are you Métis boys up to?" a brave, who appeared to be their leader said in Sioux.

"You know we are hunting buffalo, the same as our brothers the Sioux, " Beneteau said.

"Where are all your buffalo?" the Indian said, his arm making a sweeping gesture around them.

"You know they are scarce from the white men killing them for fun," Beneteau said.

"Then there aren't enough left for both Sioux and Métis," said the Sioux.

"What is your name?" said Beneteau. "I am called Hinhanska, White Owl."

"I am Black Raven, " said the Sioux.

"You aren't very well armed, Black Raven," said Beneteau. "We could smoke the pipe and talk about trading."

"We have nothing to trade," said the Indian.

"We could trade for some buffalo hunting," said Beneteau.

"We Métis know that these are hard times for Indians. This may be the last hunt we make with our carts. It isn't worth it. The herds are gone."

The Indian conferred with his warriors. "What kind of guns?" he said.

"We have some muskets at our camp. They're good Indian guns. You can make your own bullets. All you need is lead and black powder."

"How well do they shoot?" said the Indian.

"We don't have one here but Jean Baptiste can lead you back to our camp. He can explain our trade. A man called Henri Larocque will give you the guns and let you shoot them."

The Indians conferred again, then slid from their ponies and walked to where Beneteau and Jean Baptiste stood, their rifles lowered.

Beneteau fished in his saddle bags for the pipe Kicking Hawk had given him and he withdrew his pouch of tobacco. While they gathered around a new fire, Beneteau told Jean Baptiste that he hoped the Indians would go with him for the guns so he could follow the white attackers.

"We see there is blood in your camp, " Black Raven said when they were settled.

"My other friend, Ti Jacques, and I were attacked by white men here last night," said Beneteau.

"Who won?" the Indian said.

Beneteau explained Ti Jacques had a bad neck wound and the white men had fled. Now, he was after them and that was why he would not accompany the Indians to the Métis camp.

The pipe made its way around, each participant drawing in the bitter flavor of willow bark. They sealed their lips by the pipe and the smoke to speak the truth.

"We do not like the white man, but these are your enemies. We have no mind to fight them," said Black Raven. "But we understand that you must avenge your honor." What kind of gun do you have?" he said to Beneteau.

"A Henry repeating rifle. It shoots many shots by just pulling this lever. It's a good gun, but the ammunition is expensive and must be bought in stores, "Beneteau said.

"Not a good Indian gun, eh?" said Black Raven. "We know how to use muskets. How do you want to trade for buffalo?"

Beneteau suggested one rifle and 20 musket balls for each gun in exchange for ten buffalo. He also said that the Creator had made the buffalo for the Métis as well as the Indian.

"No less than five rifles for each buffalo, "said Black Raven, whose face grew stern.

"The buffalo are worth no more than one rifle for five, tops," said Beneteau.

"The guns are good," said Jean Baptiste.

"We've heard that from other traders, then learned the guns didn't even shoot," said Black Raven.

"The pipe," said Beneteau, nodding to the rawhide pouch where it had been placed beside him when they had finished smoking it. "We know its meaning, too."

The deal was struck and the braves left with Jean Baptiste, who led Ti Jacques's horse back with him. Beneteau got his gear together, saddled Bronc and set off in pursuit of the white men, whose trail he quickly picked up.

There were tracks of six horses, two of which were being led. Four riders rode abreast and the other horses trailed along behind, never breaking from their paths. Beneteau rode to near the top of a butte, stepped off Bronc and crept the rest of the way where he surveyed the terrain. He could see a wide stretch of unbroken plains with occasional hills and buttes on either side. He figured the white men would pick a trail across the flat and stick to it. He would ride abreast of what he thought was their direction to the southeast, then lie in wait when he got ahead of them.

The sun was lowering in the sky in late afternoon when Beneteau saw the dots of the attackers' movements. They would have to make camp soon. Beneteau found a watering hole and let Bronc drink and eat some grass after he loosened the girth on the saddle. The horse flicked its tail at horseflies biting its back and hips and stomped its legs to shake off the flies on its legs. Beneteau swatted at bugs, too, but his hazel eyes betrayed a man bent on a mission.

The spot the attackers picked for their camp was wide open for at least 500 yards on all sides. Beneteau studied the terrain from his prone position at the brow of a hill. He could see the sparks kick up from their campfire. They acted nervous and while one worked, two lay on the ground eying their back trail with their rifles resting on their saddles. Hunger gnawed Beneteau's insides as he watched them prepare a meal. He took a pinch of tobacco and packed it under his lower lip. It made his mouth water, but it also took his mind off eating. Beneteau was thinking the hell with it, he'd just have to charge them, but he saw the men scurry around and throw their saddles on their horses. They took off away from their camp without even dousing the fire.

Beneteau saw the silhouette shapes of five new riders. He had no idea who they might be either, except they were not Indians. When they rode into the camp of the attackers, he saw in the illumination of the campfire that one of the men was Henri Larocque and the other was Sheriff Hansen from the Turtle Mountains. He knew instantly that they were after him.

Damn Henri Larocque, he thought. Beneteau spurred Bronc to the east, but when he looked back he saw that the new riders had spotted him and were heading his way at a full gallop.

Beneteau reasoned that he had set out to avenge Ti Jacques and there was no turning back. He pointed the piebald on a southerly course by which he hoped to intercept the attackers as well as outdistance the men chasing him.

Bronc relished running and showed no sign of tiring as he sped over the ground. The cool air gushed past Beneteau's cheeks. From his throat erupted an eerie war cry that reverberated out over the prairie. Beneteau felt ancient instincts taking over his mind and body. Gone were his thoughts about the white man's religion, gone were his concerns about his relationship with Maria's father. Gone was any apprehension about right or wrong. He was like a hunter soaring in on its prey, mindful that other predators would compete with him for his chance to kill, possibly by taking his own life. Beneteau let forth another war cry into the darkness. The five riders behind him melted into the night. Coming to the top of a high hill, Beneteau pulled Bronc up to listen. And he could hear the sounds of bits and spurs jingling and pounding hoof beats somewhere ahead of him.

He pulled the Henry and levered a round into its chamber, then released the hammer to avoid accidentally firing the gun. He pushed Bronc to a gallop and headed directly toward the sounds. The attackers must have slowed their mounts in the blackness of the night because Beneteau was directly behind them in minutes. When their horses heard Bronc coming from the rear, they bolted. The riders recovered but split up and fled away from Beneteau. He singled out a rider and overrode him, unseating him with a slam from the barrel of the Henry. The man grunted when he hit the ground, but Beneteau kept charging and headed toward the next nearest rider.

That one's horse gave out, its knees buckling and casting the rider forward over its head. The man lay motionless and groaning. Beneteau could make out the forms of two more riders and he and Bronc swept toward them. Their guns flashed. The hammer of the Henry came back and Beneteau squeezed off the first round.

He levered more rounds in the chamber and fired until he was too close to use the rifle. Bronc ran up on the first horse and hit him with his chest, toppling both the man and his mount. Even in the dark, Beneteau could see the outline of the man's black beard. He leapt from Bronc's back and whirled to face his old enemy.

Blackie rolled and came up on his feet. Even in the night light, Beneteau could make out the half–moon scar on the forehead, the bushy eyebrows arched over his hard blue eyes.

"I wished I'd knowed it was you on my tail, half breed," Blackie said, sneering. "I'd of stopped and we'd settled this long ago. Cal always said I could have the first crack at you."

"You talk tough for a man about to be sent to hell," Beneteau said.

The two men edged closer to each other until they were but 15 yards apart. Both had their hands resting on the grips of their six guns.

Blackie moved first, silver revolver coming up with lightning speed. Beneteau saw the muzzle blast and felt the impact of the .45 caliber slug hit his left shoulder and spin him into a headlong fall. The Navy Colt barked in his hand as he landed on his midsection facing his assailant. Dust blasted into Beneteau's eyes from the second shot Blackie fired, narrowly missing his forehead.

Beneteau, blinded by the dirt, fired blankly in the direction of the hammer he heard being cocked in front of him. Another shot erupted, then Beneteau heard the thump of the round man's body striking the ground. Beneteau rolled, pointed the Colt at the sound again and cranked off two more rounds. With only one shot left, he lay silent and listened.

His shoulder wrenched from pain and he could feel blood oozing through his shirt. It was quiet except for the two horses snorting nearby.

Beneteau, his ears ringing from the gunfire, groped his way toward the sound of the horses until he felt Bronc's legs. He holstered his gun and worked his way up the leg and latched on with his right to a leather thong hanging from his saddle. He reached for the saddle horn and tried to mount. But his hand was ripped away and forced behind him by a stronger grip. Beneteau felt the steel of handcuffs on his wrists before the man spoke.

"This will hold you until the law can do you justice, Phillipe Beneteau, " the Turtle Mountain sheriff's voice said. "Your wild days are over."

Beneteau, who already reverted to his Indian instincts, said nothing. There was nothing to say. His game was no different than any other half breed, once someone knew he was a Métis and not white. He was at the mercy of prejudice.

"Congratulations, sheriff," Beneteau heard Henri Larocque say. "I knew you could get him. Now just take him back and see that the law punishes him for his transgressions. You can count on me to testify."

Beneteau felt one of the men with the sheriff stuff a rag against the wound in his shoulder to stem the bleeding and he was boosted on Bronc. Then, the movement, the swaying rhythm of Bronc beneath him as they led them back through the night in their own darkness. Beneteau's head bobbed over his chest. The loss of freedom was the same now as in times past. Despair overcame him. He missed the light pressure from the cross that Father Belgarde had given him.

Beneteau awoke in his small, iron, jail cell in the town of Dunseith. His wound still ached, but it was healing over having been tended to by Horace Throckmorton Bunny III, who was given permission to doctor him.

"Hinhanska, "Horace had told him, "you must now learn the white man's ways in a manner you have never done before. You will be brought to trial on charges of murdering the gold miner. You and I both know you didn't. But we need evidence. There is evidence in the will you gave to French Louis. You cannot have both Maria and your life. French Louis and Henri Larocque will get one or the other. But it is your decision."

"Old man," Beneteau had told him. "You have been trying to put me in a corner since we first met. Now, you have me where you want me."

Beneteau looked out his jail–cell window at the deep reds and oranges spreading their wings in the brightening morning sky. He had no money, no lawyer, he faced hanging and his best hope was in the witness of an aging Mandan Medicine Man who had some education by white people.

He washed his face in a basin on a wooden stool, then dried his hands. He sat on the edge of his cot and watched smoke curl slowly from the jailer's mouth as he worked over two orange crates he used for a desk in a corner of the room. The smoke wafted through an open window. Beneteau thought he, too, would be gone if he were smoke. His anguish was compounded by the loss of Ti Jacques who like Buster had moved on to the next world. His only satisfaction was in knowing that Blackie would trouble no one else. He had heard that the man called Cal had gone back to Deadwood, satisfied now that Phillipe Beneteau would pay with his life for murdering the miner. He also learned that both Cal and Blackie were land speculators, not just bent on catching him, but also interested in buying land holdings anywhere Indians had been crowded onto reservations.

The jailer rapped on his cell door with breakfast and told him he had a visitor. The jailer slid a tin bowl of oatmeal through the slit in the door, then handed him a tin cup of black coffee. Beneteau returned to his cot and was sipping the coffee when the figure loomed in the doorway to the small room in front of his cell. It was the only cell in the jail and it was housed in a small shack, behind the city hall.

"Hello, Phillipe Beneteau," said Maria Larocque. "I've been following your activities through reports from Mr. Bunny. I know about the will. I don't know what you will do about it. I do not want to follow my father's wishes that I should marry French Louis. I had to come and see you. I hope you understand."

"Your father will probably paddle your behind for coming here, " said Beneteau. She was as beautiful as ever. She had exchanged her Métis garb for a plain black neckerchief over her head and dark woolen trousers with a matching jacket draped over a purple cotton shirt.

"Jean Baptiste sends his greetings. He told me to tell you he has a plan. He is willing to come at night and break you out of jail," she said.

"That it could be so simple," Beneteau said. "You seem to forget. I have committed no crime. I don't belong in jail. I'm to be tried for something I didn't do. And Mr. Bunny knows this as well as I do. I even had a will on a piece of paper to prove it."

"Yes," Maria said. "But what you don't know is that the old man has also been arrested and will be put in jail on a charge of stealing that mule. He faces hanging, too, for riding that old mule, Opportunity."

"God," Beneteau said, sighing. "What else can go wrong? Tell Jean Baptiste I am waiting."

"Well, Phillipe Beneteau, French Louis has asked for my hand in marriage. My father told me that if I accept, French Louis says he may remember something about the miner's will that he now claims doesn't even exist."

"And you? What do you think about this?" Beneteau said hoarsely through the bars.

“I have never told you this before,” she said, reaching her hand over to where his rested on the steel of his cell. “I have fallen in love with,” her voice faltered. “With you”, she finally finished. Her dark eyes met his and he saw traces of moisture at their corners.

Before he could answer, the sheriff’s deputy entered the shack. “Times up, Miss Larocque,” he said. She turned and walked toward the door with that full–bodied gait that had tormented Beneteau before. “Goodbye, Phillipe,” she said with a sideways glance, her dark eyes hidden by the downward tilt of her head.

“Goodbye, Maria,” he said, then sat back down on his stool to consider Jean Baptiste actually helping him to break out of jail. With Horace Throckmorton Bunny III in jail, too, his future looked even worse than before.

When the guard returned, Beneteau asked where they put the old Medicine Man.

“He has been taken to Devils Lake,” the guard said. “There isn’t room here for two prisoners. Nobody wanted to see you two together anyhow. He’s lucky. Around here, folks are talking about having a necktie party to save the judge the trouble of listening to your story.”

The guard’s comments didn’t bother Beneteau more. He already knew his chances were slim because he was a breed—even with the will and Horace Throckmorton Bunny III as a witness. His hope now rested in Maria. When she told Jean Baptiste what he had said, he hoped she made it plain enough so that he would come.

Beneteau thought the plan was simple. Wait until dark, surprise the guard, get the key, let him out and make sure to bring Bronc along.

Shadows formed in the alley that ran behind the the jail and nearby house windows filled with the soft, yellow glow of kerosene lanterns. Beneteau first heard the owl hoot, then saw the movement of a man on horseback leading another. He tied up at a hitching post midway down the alley.

"Phillipe, are you in there?" Jean Baptiste finally hissed through the rear window.

"Yeah, I'm here. Get the key and let's get going."

"I'm on my way," Jean Baptiste replied.

Within two minutes he was back, "Phillipe, there's a mob forming in front of the jail and the jailer is out there trying to calm them down.

"Break down that damned back door, Jean Baptiste. The keys are hanging on a peg just inside the door to the right," Beneteau said.

This time when he returned, Beneteau heard the keys rattle in the jail door before Jean Baptiste stepped through the opening. He strode to the cell and unlocked the door and the two men burst through the back doorway and headed down the dark alley to their waiting horses. As they ran, Jean Baptiste handed Beneteau his cartridge belt and the Army Colt. "Old Henri got your rifle from the sheriff," Jean Baptiste said.

"Old Henri thinks of everything," Phillipe Beneteau said. With Bronc between his legs and loping down that alley onto the first side street before they melted into the countryside, Beneteau was thinking he should have added, "Old Henri thinks of almost everything."

As they rode along back into the ash and cottonwoods lacing the Turtle Mountains, Jean Baptiste mentioned Horace Throckmorton Bunny III. "Do you suppose we ought to let that old man hang for stealing that mule?"

Beneteau had been thinking that Horace was now a relative and wasn't any more guilty of a crime than he was.

"I suppose we'll have to try to do something about him, too," Beneteau said.

When they got to the village, Beneteau left Bronc staked in the dark and rode double with Jean Baptiste. He dropped off at Koohkoum Emma's. Jean Baptiste was told to find Maria and bring her.

Koohkoum Emma looked up and smiled when she saw her grandson enter the cabin behind his familiar knock. "I knew you would be coming," she said. "Let me fix you something to eat." She dropped her sewing cloth over the back of a chair and began rattling pots and pans in her kitchen space. She poured him a cup of black coffee.

"I simply couldn't believe my eyes when they come for Horace," she said. "Henri Larocque has gone crazy. They say he even tried to get the sheriff to take Ti Jacques because he was with you. The buffalo hunt ended when the sheriff got you," she said.

The knock at the door startled Beneteau, but he calmed quickly when he heard Jean Baptiste's voice. "Come out back, Phillipe," he said softly. Beneteau quickly glided to the back door and entered the brisk night air. He saw Jean Baptiste moving around the corner of the house, then the smaller form of a woman, Maria.

She leapt toward him, throwing her arms around his neck and pressing her lips firmly against his, almost before he could get his own arms to move. Then, he grabbed her firmly by her thin waist and slid his hands up the small of her back and brought her to him.

“Hey, hey, you two,” said Jean Baptiste. Don’t forget we have a lot of work and riding to do.”

Maria told them she would hide the Henry rifle her father had taken at the rear of their chicken coop. Give her about 15 minutes. Before she left, she turned to Beneteau and said, “I don’t know what your plans are, but you better figure me into them because I’ll be there one way or the other.”

Chapter 14

The two Métis men eyed the front of the Devils Lake jail from a corner of the busy main street where they stood looking at a set of horse harness hanging from a rafter in front of a small hardware store.

"You boys planning to buy something?" the storeowner said, eying Jean Baptiste suspiciously.

"We're checking out your used harness," Beneteau said. "How much?"

"About $15," the shopkeeper said. "I'll throw in a pair of neck collars for $4 more." It was late afternoon.

"We'll look around a bit more," Beneteau told him. They walked away from the direction of the jail.

"How do suppose we'll find out where Mr. Bunny is in there?" Jean Baptiste said.

"I guess we can't send you in there, so I'll have to go," Beneteau said.

"That's pretty risky, Phillipe. They might know you broke out of jail in Dunseith. They'll be on the lookout."

"It's a risk we have to take or we wouldn't be here," Beneteau said. "Nobody should be too excited about an old man who only stole a mule."

They walked to where they had their horses hobbled at the edge of town in some trees where they ate some dried meat and hard bread Maria had given them. As the shadows lengthened into darkness, Beneteau explained to Jean Baptiste how to ride through the jail alley after he entered the building. If he and Horace Throckmorton Bunny III were not through the alley door by the time the horses crossed the path of the back doorway, Jean Baptiste was to ride on past and wait at this spot until Beneteau returned.

Beneteau's boots echoed hollowly on the boardwalk as he approached the sheriff's office, now basking in the glow of a kerosene lantern.

"Evening," he said to the jailer when he entered the building.

"Can I help you?" the deputy said.

"Yes sir," Beneteau said. "I just stopped in to see if I could check your wanted posters. A friend of mine up north said he thought he saw a man wanted for bank robbery the other day."

"What'd he say his name was," the jailer said. He turned to his desk to retrieve a pile of posters hanging on a spike.

"He didn't say, just said the man wore a long moustache and beard."

"Got to be a hundred of them," the jailer said. "But here take a look."

Beneteau thumbed through the posters, then saw there were three cells at the rear of the room. Horace Throckmorton Bunny III sat eying him in the cell closest to the doorway.

"Sorry about this," Beneteau said, handing the posters back to the jailer and pulling his Army Colt at the same time. "Just hand me the keys to that cell and keep moving and nothing will happen."

"Hinhanska, I didn't think you could come," Horace said when he came out of the cell.

"We'll talk later," Beneteau said, pushing the jailer into the cell. Beneteau cut a piece of cloth from the blanket on the cell cot and bound it around the jailer's mouth, then tied his hands behind his back. He closed the door and nudged Horace to the back door, which he opened slowly.

No one was in sight. Beneteau stepped into the darkness and peered up and down the alley. Jean Baptiste had either not got there yet or had already passed by. "Come on," he said to Horace and they slipped out of the jail after gently closing the door behind them. They could hear the jailer thrashing about in the cell through the walls.

The two moved quietly down the alley in the dark until they came to the first street. Beneteau estimated it to be a quarter of a mile to where he and Jean Baptiste had kept their horses.

"How fast can you move?" he said to Horace.

"You've seen me move before, Hinhanska," the old man said. "I'm not any faster than I was before. And I'm hungry."

"If you hadn't stolen that mule, you wouldn't be in this trouble," Beneteau whispered. He took Horace's arm and they walked quickly across the street which was lit by a gas lantern hanging on a pole. Then they melted into the darkness again.

"I didn't steal Opportunity. You know that," said Horace, who was already breathing hard.

“And I didn’t steal that old miner’s gold,” said Beneteau. A dog barked at them from behind a wooden fence. Then a man’s voice growled from a back door that was thrown open. “What are you barking at, Rex? Shut up or you’ll wake the whole neighborhood.” The animal followed along the fence as the two men passed outside, the dog growling until they were well away from its territory.

As they moved from the center of town, the lights were fewer and the night darker and more silent. Only their footsteps rasped on the ground. Beneteau led the Medicine Man out of the alley and down a street which was speckled with light from only a couple of house windows and then they were at the edge of town.

Jean Baptiste has the horses. He was supposed to meet us at the back door,” Beneteau told Horace.

The old man mumbled inaudibly in the dark until Beneteau stopped and asked what he was doing.

“I’m praying to the Creator,” Horace said. “It is plain to me that I’m going to need more help than you are giving. Not that I’m not thankful that you got me out of that jail.”

“Well, you keep praying and I’ll keep looking for Jean Baptiste,” Beneteau said. “This won’t be going well if we don’t find him pretty soon.”

Beneteau hooted like an owl, but heard no answer. The two crouched in the blackness while Horace Throckmorton Bunny III continued his low chanting.

“Damn it, would you stop that,” Beneteau said finally.

“Hinhanska,” the old man said. “Hold your tongue. We are both in need of a response from the Creator, who knows that you and your friend Jean Baptiste have good hearts but minds that need rebuilding. If a plan as simple as yours has fallen apart, what do think the future portends? I, a simple man of prayer, am deeply enmeshed in your foolishness.”

Beneteau heard a noise in the darkness and the Colt was back in his hand, the hammer signaling its readiness with a metal double clicking. Then, total silence again. "Must have been a four–legged critter," he mumbled to himself.

"It is not all bad news," Horace whispered to him in the dark. "I heard one night when we made our way back from that dismal hunting trip that Maria's father was given the miner's will in down payment for her marriage to French Louis."

"I would never have thought Henri was such a bastard," said Beneteau.

"Nor I," said Horace. "We should pray for him, but if we can't sway him with prayer, you must go to Koohkoum Emma's cart and retrieve my small guns. I hung them in a bag on the underside of the cart box at the axle."

"Old man, you are always full of surprises. But in the end, you are no different than I am. First we pray for the best, then we take matters into our own hands."

"It is not wise, Hinhanska. But it is the way of our world. Your priest started to hound Koohkoum Emma and me to get married properly by him. He does not seem to understand our ways. At our age, just being together is holy."

"Did they get your mule?" Beneteau asked.

"That accursed animal ran away while we were still on the hunt. He followed the camp at a distance and no one even tried to catch him for me. As far as I know, he returned to the Turtle Mountains and is running loose in the hills."

An owl hooted off in the distance. Beneteau answered. The next hoot was closer but still far enough away so that Beneteau left Horace and silently moved in the direction from which the last sound came. He saw the darker forms of horses and a rider first, then heard the hooves scuffing on the ground.

"Jean Baptiste," Beneteau said in a low voice.

"Phillipe, over here," he heard the big man reply.

"Where in hell were you?" Beneteau said when they came together.

"Gees, I'm sorry, Phillipe. I must have got the directions mixed up. I followed the alleys through the whole town and never saw nothing. Then, I circled around the outskirts back here. Even this meeting place is hidden like a bird's nest in the grass."

"C'mon," said Beneteau. "We've got to get Mr. Bunny and us out of here. We've a long ways to go before dawn. They might be forming up to look for us right now."

Beneteau mounted Bronc, then grabbed Horace and swung him up behind. "Hang on, Mr. Bunny," he told the old man who he felt clinging to him rigidly with both arms. They put their horses to a lope and headed into night. They stayed clear of the main road, but kept to a northerly course. Beneteau handed the old man the last half of a sandwich and he freed one arm to wolf it down. Then, he asked for a drink of water.

"Why did you come for me, Hinhanska?" Horace asked finally when he had slaked his thirst.

"That's a good question. Hey, Jean Baptiste, do you know why we came to get Mr. Bunny?"

Jean Baptiste said from his horse gently rocking along side of Bronc. "We're just kind of goofy Métis boys with nothing to do, I guess."

Beneteau smiled in the darkness. He knew he would never have been able to face Koohkoum Emma again if they hadn't at least tried to get the old man out of jail.

"You really need my spiritual guidance, Hinhanska, " Horace said.

"I guess so," said Beneteau. "Have you got any idea what we should do now? We're wanted men and they'll be looking for us for escaping from jail, murder and horse thieving."

"Gees, Phillipe, I didn't do any of that," said Jean Baptiste.

"You're an accomplice now," Beneteau said.

"Does that mean I have to be on the run, too?"

"Yep, I'm afraid so, friend."

"Life was simple for me until I took on caring for your spiritual well being," said Horace.

"I never asked it of you," said Beneteau. "I always thought you wanted to go back to your people on the Missouri River."

"I planned on it, but a woman has a way of changing even the best man's mind," the old man said.

The night was filled with more blackness than anything else, but the stars were still brilliant in the sky. Coyotes yipped a bit from nearby hill tops and now and then a night owl screeched.

The sun brightened the east sky when they viewed the Métis camp in the Turtle Mountains after a two–day ride.

Beneteau pulled Bronc up in a clump of chokecherry bushes beginning to sprout leaves. He let Horace use his foot to step down from the horse, then he followed suit. All three men stood looking through the branches at the small settlement, smoke curling skyward from chimneys. Dogs and children ran through the pathways that separated log dwellings among which were tipis and other tents. Beneteau's wound was acting up, but he drove the pain of it from his mind.

"The first place they look for us will be here," Beneteau said. "We've got to make contact, somehow, but not let every

one know we're back—especially Henri." Beneteau watched some women walking slowly toward the creek to fetch water.

"Jean Baptiste, see if you can get down there close enough to get somebody's attention. You are the least wanted of us. If you have any trouble, I'll come in and help you. This is where we will meet again."

"Who should I look for?" Jean Baptiste said.

"You might try my beloved Koohkoum Emma," said Horace. "The only other person I've seen you two get along with at all is Maria, but contacting her could be dangerous."

"Tell whoever you talk to that we need supplies and we have to pick them up tonight by the spring above the camp. Go now and stay out of trouble."

"Hinhanska, we can't ride together forever," Horace said, as Jean Baptiste and his horse left and picked their way through edge of the birch and cottonwood trees to the small stream below. "Why didn't you tell him we will need horses, too?"

"None of us has an extra horse," said Beneteau. "And we're sure not going to steal them from our own people."

"I won't travel with you anywhere without Koohkoum Emma," the Medicine Man said.

"Suit yourself," Beneteau said. "But you are a wanted man and I won't be breaking you out of jail again."

Beneteau decided to ride a circle around the camp to make sure no one had pursued them this far yet. He left Horace Throckmorton Bunny III to keep an eye on the camp from their lookout. The trails he followed were familiar haunts and he felt perfectly at home as Bronc stepped lightly along the damp silent forest roads. If one watched the blackbirds and jays, or the forest floor for four–leggeds, one could read quickly the movement of others before meeting them. As he rode, Beneteau saw animal movement was away from him. He decided to visit the spring that was to be used for a meeting place at night.

Beneteau dismounted when he got to the pool of clear water. He loosened his grip on the reins to let Bronc take a long drink. The trees were alive with jays and robins darting to the water, then back up in the tree limbs. Beneteau walked the perimeter of the spring, noticing as he went the prints of deer, coon and squirrels pressed in the mud. On the far side, he saw the rounded hoof prints of a horse. He dropped on the ground and scooped water into his hands to drink himself. Then, instinctively leading Bronc, Beneteau dropped back into the edged of the trees where they stopped again to look around.

While they rested in the quiet, Beneteau was brought alert by twigs snapping. Bronc's ears perked, too.

"What is it, boy?" Beneteau said quietly, as he withdrew the Henry from its scabbard. Beneteau, hunched at the waist, moved silently toward the sound. He parted the willows in front of him with the barrel of the rifle, then relaxed with a chuckle. Opportunity stood grazing in a clearing, a short chunk of lead rope still dangling from it's halter.

"Whoa, there old timer," Beneteau told the mule, who edged away from him when he tried to approach on foot. The mule turned its rear toward him, then started to amble back into the brush. When Beneteau stopped, the mule did, too. But if he came at him, the mule persisted in staying out of range of the man's arms. Finally, Beneteau returned to where he had Bronc tied.

The mule stood fast when he saw the horse coming and Beneteau scooped up the short rope and dropped down beside the mule. "You're sure an ornery cuss," he said, stroking the animal's neck.

Opportunity let out a bray that sounded like a monster was loosed in the woods. "Jesus, won't you shut up?" Beneteau said. "You'll tell the whole damned country where we are." The mule brayed again. Beneteau fashioned a lead rope from his rawhide lariat and joined it to the halter rope.

They then set out to get back to Horace Throckmorton Bunny III.

The Medicine Man was snoozing when they arrived. Beneteau walked Opportunity to where Horace lie on some brush piled behind a downed log. He tied the mule to the log, unsaddled Bronc to let him graze, then sat down and leaned against a tree. His eyes slipped shut and he dozed.

"What is this?" Horace said, when Opportunity finally realized he was going no where and might as well renew their friendship. The mule pushed his soft nose right into the side of Horace's face, slobbering over him and munching his cheek.

"Oh my, god," the old man said, shaking his head and wiping his eyes. "It looks like I get to have more of the white man's Opportunity."

The commotion awakened Beneteau, too, who eyed the two with a smile on his lips.

While Horace and the mule renewed their friendship, Beneteau took up a position at the edge of a rock cliff from which he could observe anyone coming. After a couple of hours passed, he got anxious, saddled Bronc and told the old man he would ride in closer to learn what was holding up Jean Baptiste.

The two men met half the distance from the meeting spot.

"Phillipe, over here," said Jean Baptiste when he saw Beneteau, who had been watching silently as the big man approached.

"Well, what's up?" Beneteau said as they drew within speaking distance of each other.

"I sent word through to Koohkoum Emma that we would be coming in at dark for supplies."

Beneteau told him that they may have a change in plans. That instead of packing supplies on their horses, they should hitch her cart to the ox and bring her along if she wanted to come.

"She is an old woman," Jean Baptiste said. "Won't she slow us down, Phillipe?"

Beneteau said that they already were slowed by Horace Throckmorton Bunny III and that he wouldn't budge if they didn't bring her, too.

"Well, whatever you say, Phillipe. I just hope we get to moving. What are we going to do?"

"It doesn't look like we have much choice," Beneteau said. "I believe we might as well head for Canada and take up with our Métis cousins on the other side of the border."

The two men rode silently back to where Horace was waiting for them.

By nightfall, they were picking their way down the trail leading to the camp. Horace had redressed Beneteau's shoulder wound and daubed it with the paste he made from his herbal bundle. Whatever it was worked and Beneteau felt healed.

The trio slipped into the camp and rode to where livestock were penned. Beneteau rode Bronc among the cattle until he found Koohkoum Emma's black ox, which he roped with his lariat. They led the big animal along the back side of the camp until they were behind his grandmother's log dwelling.

Beneteau dismounted and walked through the backyard to her door. He listened for voices, then opened the door and stepped inside. She looked up and emitted a gasp, then walked quickly to him and threw her arms around him.

“Phillipe Beneteau,” she said, “I am so happy to see you.”

He told her of their plan and that the other two were outside waiting in the dark. Koohkoum Emma said she had stacked all the buffalo meat she had dried from the hunt, along with flour and beans in the small shed out back. The cart was there, too.

While she packed some clothing in a grain sack, Beneteau and Jean Baptiste hitched the ox and loaded the supplies. Horace disappeared into the house, then came out with the bundle of clothing hung over his shoulder and Koohkoum Emma holding onto his hand.

“We don’t want to be wasting any time here, “ Beneteau said. “Let’s load and get going.”

Within 15 minutes they were moving, the wheels from the cart emitting a cranky squeal that sent chills up Beneteau’s spine. He only could hope that the wind, which was dying, muffled the sound of their departure. Opportunity brought up the rear where he had been tied to the cart.

Beneteau could not resist the temptation to contact Maria. He told Jean Baptiste, then loped Bronc out of sight in the direction of Henri Larocque’s home.

Lantern light was streaming from the Larocque windows when he stepped off Bronc and crept toward the house.

Henri Larocque sat in the light polishing a rifle stock. Beneteau could not see Maria in the room and was about to leave when he saw movement in the kitchen. He waited. Maria appeared with two cups of coffee, one of which she gave to her father who set it on a hand--hewn wooden chair while he continued to clean his rifle. Maria sat opposite him and after sipping from her coffee, began to mend a shirt.

Beneteau rose with his face in the window. He imagined that he might look monstrous in the gleam of the lantern.

Maria started when she saw him, then quickly composed herself and looked back down at the shirt she was working on. Beneteau stepped slowly away from the window and waited. He saw Maria's lips move and her father nod slightly without looking up. Then, she got up and left the room.

Beneteau heard the front door to the house open and close, then she was by his side, her arms thrown around his neck and her hands pulling his head to hers where their lips met. She felt warm and soft against his body. He felt a tinge of pain in his shoulder but ignored it as they embraced.

"Oh my god, Phillipe Beneteau," she said, gasping for air. "I thought I'd never see you again."

Beneteau told her there wasn't much time, but he was free and would soon be heading to Canada with the others.

Maria told him that she had learned that her father had the old miner's will and had agreed to allow someone to rediscover it once she and French Louis were married.

"I don't think the justice I've seen would even take it into account, " he told her. "A breed isn't given much of a chance. And a breed whose best witness is an old Indian even less. You are Métis, too," he told her.

"French Louis has said I would be welcome in Devils Lake," she said. "We'd have a fine house and I could even have a maid."

"Maria, all my life I've been able to pass as a white man. I've heard what they have to say when they think no one is listening. You can fool yourself for a while, but in the end you and I are a mixture that the world isn't ready for yet. You can do what you want. I just wanted to see you before we leave."

"Maria," Henri Larocque shouted through the door before he flung it open. "Are you out there with somebody?" As his silhouette filled the doorway, Beneteau slipped deeper into the shadows.

"No, Papa, I am just watching the stars," she said.

"You better get in here. It's pretty soon time for bed and you still have work to do." he said.

"I'll be along in a few moments," she said.

Beneteau stepped back when the door shut and he took her in his arms and kissed her again. "Goodbye, Maria," he said. "You have been a dream I've had for a long time. I have to go now." Emptiness gushed into him as his hand slipped away from hers and they parted.

"Goodbye, Phillipe Beneteau," she said, softly. He heard the door close behind him as he retreated into the darkness.

The sun was coming up through the trees and tops of the Turtle Mountains. The ox was just slow and steady and Beneteau worried that they would soon be overtaken. He dispatched Jean Baptiste to check their back trail after they paused for coffee. Koohkoum Emma cut slices of homemade dark bread, which she passed out with pieces of buffalo meat. The meat had been boiled in a brass pot on a small fire made by Beneteau and fueled by Horace Throckmorton Bunny III.

"Hinhanska," the old man said while Koohkoum Emma packed the few breakfast tools back in the pot, "let me see that wound."

Beneteau slipped off his rawhide shirt and exposed the bandage on his shoulder. Horace cut the cloth with his knife and peeled it back. The gash was healed, although there was a purplish lump where the bullet had exited at his back.

"I have not lost my touch," the Medicine Man said. He ran his bony fingers over the wound and pressed it. "No pain, eh, " he said to Beneteau whose eyes he had watched.

"No pain," said Beneteau. "What did you have in that concoction?

"Normally, I wouldn't say. But you need to be told many things to bring you around. I mixed a paste of buffalo dung. We've always used buffalo dung, but the white man doesn't think it works. I don't think we need another bandage."

Beneteau was in awe of the native doctor. But he worried more that they were being followed as he pulled his shirt back over his head. Opportunity stood grazing with Bronc and the ox. He took the ox yoke and approached the wary mule.

"Steady boy," he said. "I have to find out if you are willing to do an honest day's work." He reached for the mule's halter, then brought the leather collar up around its neck. Opportunity, it appeared, had been driven in his time. Beneteau led the mule to the pulling harness, strapped the hames over the collar and fitted the croup under his tail. With reins in hand, Beneteau snapped Opportunity on the rump. The mule responded by stepping off smartly. "You'll do," Beneteau said. He drove the mule over the wagon shafts and backed him to the hitch.

"He's all yours," Beneteau said to Horace, tossing him the reins after the old man and Koohkoum Emma had settled on their cart seat.

"Let's go, you infernal demon," Horace said. The mule moved away at a smooth trot. Beneteau followed and the ox tried to keep up rather than be left behind in the forest, perhaps sensing he might become a meal for bears.

Within five miles of their travel, Jean Baptiste caught up with them.

"We've got company coming behind us," he told Beneteau.

Chapter 15

Beneteau told Horace to keep the mule going north while he and Jean Baptiste checked out who was after them.

"Be careful, Phillipe," Koohkoum Emma said as the two Métis men rode away.

"Emma, it is we who must be careful. They can take care of themselves," Horace said. "Opportunity sometimes acts like he has a mind of his own." The cart screeched and lurched forward. But its five-foot wheels kept it well above obstacles to the undercarriage.

"You ride on the left and I'll take the right," Beneteau told Jean Baptiste. "If you see them, signal, get on the ground and we'll catch them in a crossfire."

The two worked their way along the trail until they came to a small, grassy valley they had passed through. Beneteau called a halt at the tree line and they dismounted and tied their horses.

With Henry in hand, Beneteau took up a position behind a group of granite boulders perched on the hillside. Jean Baptiste dropped down behind a tangle of deadfall opposite him and they waited.

Four riders bobbed into view at the other edge of the valley. As they neared, Beneteau made out that two of them were Henri Larocque and Sheriff Hansen and the other two were probably deputies.

Beneteau signaled to Jean Baptiste to hold his fire until they were within range.

The five riders moved at a trot toward them as Beneteau raised his rifle, chambered a round and nodded at Jean Baptiste. The air erupted with bullets whizzing past the riders heads and they dove from their horses to the ground.

"Hold your fire, hold your fire," the sheriff shouted.

Beneteau nodded at Jean Baptiste again and they fired another volley toward the deposed riders.

"Phillipe Beneteau," Henri Larocque shouted. "Is that you?"

"And what if it is?" Beneteau replied.

"We've come to make a deal," said Henri.

"I'm listening," said Beneteau. "Show yourself."

"Turn yourself in," said Henri without moving. "All the others can go free."

"Turn myself in for what?" Beneteau said.

"For the murder of that old miner," Henri said. "You'll be given a fair trial, but you must turn yourself in."

"You already know that I didn't kill that miner," Beneteau shouted back.

"You must prove that in court," said the sheriff. "If you are innocent, you shall be found innocent."

Beneteau sensing a trap looked over at Jean Baptiste who was watching their left flank. Beneteau saw his friend raise his rifle and sight along its barrel to a point in the woods.

He panned the woods with his Henry. Smoke exploded from gunfire on both sides. The leaves shattered and flew in all directions. Lead kicked up dirt all around both Métis men and the four riders in front of them also fired.

Beneteau and Jean Baptiste emptied their rifles.

"Jean Baptiste, back," Beneteau shouted to his friend. He watched the big man rise as a new volley erupted from the trees. Cursing under his breath, Beneteau joined the retreat. They zig–zagged their way to where the horses were tethered. Beneteau rolled up on Bronc, whose legs clawed at the earth to escape the trees splintered around them. The air hissed. Beneteau rode low over Bronc's left shoulder. He peered back and saw men running from the trees and firing at them as Jean Baptiste's horse buckled under him. Bronc wound down the hill, but Beneteau reined him across its midsection and they emerged at the top again just in time to see the big guy back in the saddle and plunging to safety behind the hill. Beneteau followed.

"Jean Baptiste, stay on the trail," he yelled at his friend. "I'll lead them away."

There was no point in going after Horace and Koohkoum Emma. The men were after him. He pulled Bronc up when they were out of range of the rifle fire. Beneteau reloaded the Henry kept on a parallel course the old people were taking with the cart, but he would circle through the hills before coming back in front of them. He wasn't worried that the hunters would get him. They wouldn't have got close to any of them if not for Henri Larocque's treachery.

Beneteau halted Bronc and slipped from his back to the soft, damp forest floor. He tossed his flat-brimmed hat to the ground and ripped off his rawhide tunic. From his saddle bag, he withdrew a beaded headband into which he placed the eagle feather from his hat. He fell on his knees and began to cry a death song to his Creator.

"One Above, I have tried to walk honorably."

"You Who see all have watched my life."

"I can no longer follow this crooked trail."

"One Above, I am ready to come to You."

The anger of revenge filled his eyes. Phillipe Beneteau transformed from the Golden Métis to Hinhanska the White Owl. He daubed mud under his eyes and made black streaks down his cheeks. Across his forehead, he drew a zig-zagging line. He would now fly the erratic flight of the White Owl in search of his prey. The black lines reflected his thoughts, now only of killing and death. His last act of preparation was to bind himself physically and spiritually to Bronc by placing his muddy hand behind his left shoulder where the piebald's heart was.

"We go now to the nothing from which we came, brother," he spoke softly to the big horse, who danced under his legs and leaned his long neck forward in anticipation of the gentle squeeze he would feel from White Owl's lean, muscular legs.

It came and the big horse tightened, then careened into motion, banging his glistening shoulders and flanks into the white birch saplings to either side of them. They emerged into the sun like a dream come to life. The white body, the blackened face, the streaming long ponytail dancing behind the warrior's straight shoulders. Hinhanska rode with his Henry pointed skyward. His hazel eyes raked the terrain in front and behind. He missed the wood cross of his childhood dangling from his neck. Horse and man pressed forward in the hope of overtaking the old people in the cart and Jean Baptiste before turning back to meet the hunters in combat.

Dark clouds rolled in by the wind began to send their grey trails of rain to the earth. The first drops sent a shiver up Beneteau's spine, then he put the Henry back into its scabbard as the intensity increased. Thunder banged around the black clouds and the driving rain glistened in brilliant flashes of lightning.

Bronc lowered his proud head and laid his ears back to avoid the rain and Beneteau saw the mud from his own body forming black rivulets down his muscular abdomen. He could feel Bronc's legs groping to keep upright until he knew he had to dismount and walk with the horse. They plodded on, water washing them clean. Beneteau now thought only of getting to the old people, who he knew were also being pummeled by the storm. He changed his course in the hope of intersecting their route more directly.

The cart appeared first as a blob of grey that seemed unnatural in the wooded setting but began to take a more familiar shape with harsher lines when Beneteau and Bronc stumbled forward. It seemed abandoned, but Opportunity stood hunched up nearby, long ears flattened, huddled by the side of the ox.

Beneteau tied Bronc to a wheel, then checked around. The old people had vanished. He unsaddled Bronc and tossed the saddle under the cart. He led the horse to the other two animals and hobbled him. To get some relief from the rain, he crawled under the cart and fetched his rawhide shirt from the saddlebag. He stretched it on, then leaned against the saddle to watch the storm. Treetops rocked in the howling wind and water built in gullies as it descended to the next level below. He noticed the bag dangling from the axle where Horace kept his guns.

A faint glow on the side of a hill was the first sign to Beneteau that he was not completely alone. He stared at it as it pulsated dimly through the rain. Lightning washed it away, but the light reappeared in the darkness.

Beneteau grabbed the Henry and slipped and slid along a deer path toward the light. A humming sound came to his ears and ignited his hopes. The light grew stronger and Beneteau sensed it was coming from a cave carved by erosion in an outcrop of sandstone looming before him.

"Hinhanska, we were worried about you," said Horace Throckmorton Bunny III when Beneteau stepped into light and warmth emitting from the cave entrance.

Koohkoum Emma dropped her stirring stick into the pot hanging over the fire and gave him a big hug.

"You must be starved, Phillipe," she said. "Where is Jean Baptiste?"

"He was supposed to be here with you," said Beneteau. He told them of the ambush.

"They were after me and unless this storm slowed them they still are," he said.

Koohkoum Emma gave him a bowl of steaming buffalo stew, which he savored so quickly she had to fill the bowl again before he spoke.

"Hinhanska, even the animals know that weather like this isn't fit for travel. Get some rest. I'll tend to your animal when I tend to ours," said Horace.

Beneteau fell into a deep sleep on a buffalo robe on the floor. When he opened his eyes again, Horace was coming into the cave with an armload of firewood. His robe was dusted white. Day was breaking and the storm continued in the form of snow.

"The animals are fine," the old man said. "The Creator has taken care of them. Both Opportunity and your horse are pawing through the snow to the grass and the ox is grazing with them. I pulled them down a couple of young cottonwood trees. They'll be fine. They have plenty of snow to drink."

"Any sign of that bunch that was after us?" Beneteau said.

"No," said Horace. "Nothing is moving out there. They'll be lucky if they got out before the rain turned to snow. Besides, I think we are in Canada."

"If they are gone, I want to go back and look for Jean Baptiste," Beneteau said.

"Yes, Hinhanska. We'll help you when the storm lets up," Horace said. "This reminds me of when I was boy."

Koohkoum Emma put another piece of wood on the fire, stirring sparks that lifted to the low ceiling. She sat at the fire with her legs to one side, her dark eyes glistening in the light.

"Tell us of when you were a boy," she said.

"We lived on the Missouri River where the white man's boats were steaming by. We trapped and hunted and the women raised squash and corn in their big gardens. And we lived in round earth lodges."

"In winter we ate the food we had stored in Mother Earth and the buffalo we dried. The lodges were big enough even for our horses. Our fires were at the center of the lodge, brightening our lives as Father Sun did outside."

"The old men and women told stories. We learned about Lone Man and the Great Canoe he came in after the flood. I had doubts about the stories, but when the whites took me away and taught their religion, I learned about Noah and the Ark and how he had loaded all the animals before the Creator sent the flood waters over the whole earth. Maybe Noah was Lone Man."

"Strange," said Horace, "us being brought together in this cave, eating the Sacred Buffalo before the fire—our animals outside and protected by the gifts the Creator gave them."

While the old people chatted, Beneteau rose to check outside. The wind seemed to be settling down and visibility was improving. He stepped through the cave entrance and stretched, for he had to bend over when he stood up in the cave.

It felt good to be free and to breathe the fresh air. The woods around them were quiet except for the snow drifting in meandering paths until being caught on a brush pile. He looked down and again felt empty without the wooden cross hanging from his neck, but even more so at the loss of Maria. He went back inside the cave and sat down in the warmth and companionship of his grandmother and new grandfather.

"Koohkoum Emma, will you come with me to check on our animals?" Horace said to her.

"I can take care of them," Beneteau said.

"You need to rest," said Koohkoum. "We need to get some fresh air."

They left and Beneteau sorted through his belongings, few as they were tucked in his saddle bags. He got the Henry and cleaned and oiled it.

Beneteau started at the first two shots. By the time, he sprang through the cave entrance, two more shots were fired.

Beneteau sprinted to the top of the first rise on the trail back to the animals as the shooting stopped amidst an eerie calm, broken only by the shout of a man's voice.

"I'm coming in," said the voice of Jean Baptiste.

Beneteau dropped behind a bush and saw first Bronc then the other two animals standing in the snow. Nearby were Koohkoum Emma and Horace Throckmorton Bunny III, his Derringers both drawn.

Beneteau's roared with laughter when he stood up. "What are you guys shooting at?" he said.

"I saw Jean Baptiste coming with someone and when he stopped to fire his signal shots, I answered it was okay here," said Horace.

Beneteau watched the two riders pick their way to where the animals and old people stood. He jogged down the trail and stood waiting as the riders approached. Beneteau's stomach knotted up and a lump got stuck in his throat. The rider with Jean Baptiste was Maria.

"What brings you into the woods?" he said to her as she and Jean Baptiste stepped off their horses.

Maria dropped the reins and ran to Beneteau, her arms draping him in an embrace. Beneteau tilted her head upward and pressed his lips firmly against hers before she answered. Her wet hair formed as rivulets down her cheeks.

"I guess she just followed her dad and the sheriff," Jean Baptiste said. "I bumped into her after I left you, Phillipe."

"I overheard what they were planning to do," said Maria. "I tried to warn you but it was too late. I heard the shooting."

Beneteau gave her another hug. "Are you coming with us, then?" he said.

"Of course," she said. "It will take years for Papa to get over this, my going with you. But I've made up my mind." Maria reached in her jacket pocket and brought out Beneteau's cross. She said one of the last requests Ti Jacques had made was to see to it Phillipe got his cross back.

Beneteau slipped the cross back over his neck, then warned the others to pack up. "We might be in Canada right now," he said, but not very far."

Within a half hour, the old people were loaded on their cart and they.winded their way through the snow deeper into the north country.

"Where might we be heading?" Horace said.

"I was thinking Batoche, eventually," Beneteau said. "I remember somebody saying they thought that was where my folks might have gone."

"Batoche," said Koohkoum Emma. "That has a nice sound to it. I hear there are many Métis people there. We should be safe."

Later that day, the sheriff said to Henri Larocque as the two men looked at the trail heading north, that the small group had one left. "I guess you just have to face it, Henri, he got away."

Without looking back, the group turned to the south. Henri Larocque took a small, brown piece of paper from his shirt pocket. He unfolded it and read the shaky handwriting of its author, an unknown miner. He tore it in half, then again until it was just a handful of tidbits which he tossed to the side of the trail. French Louis would have to make a new deal for Maria, he thought.

Unnoticed above them, the bright, yellow eyes of a snow owl peered down from the branch of a towering aspen tree. When the riders passed, the owl screeched to the other forest creatures.

Then, the white owl just sat and stared in silence at the group of men and horses departing.

Flynn J. Ell

is a retired newsman who worked on newspapers in Minnesota, Montana, North Dakota and Washington.

He was introduced 20 years ago to the term Métis through Montana historian Joseph Kinsey Howard's "*Strange Empire*," a history of Louis Riel's tragic efforts to provide a land base for his people.

Prior to that time there were only three kinds of people in his life. They were Indian, white or half breeds.

Ell, his wife Karin and a few animals live in the country west of Killdeer, ND. His ancestry is a mix of French Canadian, Irish and German from Russia and includes direct lines to about 20 of Quebec's first French families, a number of whom show marriages within Indian tribes.
He is also one of the many descendants of Pierre Couc, a French soldier/interpreter who married the Abenaki woman Marie "Swamp Medicine" Miteouamigoukoue on April 16, 1657, at St. Maurice, Trois Rivieres, Quebec.

Through the wonders of genealogy by computer, Ell found he even shares a great grandfather, Marin Boucher, with Louis Riel.

The *Golden Métis* is his second novel after *Dakota Scouts*, Walker & Co., N.Y., N.Y.,1992.